D1394888

RAFFAELE: TAMING HIS TEMPESTUOUS VIRGIN

RAFFAELE: TAMING HIS TEMPESTUOUS VIRGIN

BY

SANDRA MARTON

MILLS & BOON

First published in Great Britain 2009
Large Print edition 2010
Harlequin Mills & Boon Limited,
Eton House, 18-24 Paradise Road,
Richmond, Surrey TW9 1SR

© Sandra Myles 2009

ISBN: 978 0 263 21181 8

Harlequin Mills & Boon policy is to use papers that are
natural, renewable and recyclable products and made
from wood grown in sustainable forests. The logging and
manufacturing process conform to the legal environmental
regulations of the country of origin.

Printed and bound in Great Britain
by CPI Antony Rowe, Chippenham, Wiltshire

CHAPTER ONE

RAFFAELE ORSINI prided himself on being a man who was always in control. There was no doubt that his ability to separate emotion from logic was one reason he'd come this far in life.

Rafe could look at a relatively nondescript investment bank or financial corporation and see not what it was but what it could be, given time and money and, of course, the expert guidance he and his brothers could provide. They had created Orsini Brothers only five years ago but they were already an incredible success in the high-stakes world of international finance.

They'd always been incredibly successful with beautiful women.

The brothers shared the dark good looks of their mother and the rapier-sharp intellect of their father, who'd both immigrated to the States from Sicily decades before. Unlike their old man, they'd put their talents into lawful pursuits, but there was a dangerous edge to them that worked to their advantage in bedrooms as well as boardrooms.

It had done so today, when Rafe had outbid a Saudi prince for the purchase of a venerable French bank the Orsinis had wanted for a very long time. He, Dante, Falco and Nicolo had celebrated with drinks a couple of hours ago.

A perfect day, on its way to becoming a perfect evening...

Until now.

Rafe stepped from the lobby of his mistress's apartment building—his *former* mistress's apartment building, he thought coldly—declined the doorman's offer of a taxi and dragged in a deep breath of cool autumn air. He needed to calm down. Maybe the walk from Sutton Place to his Fifth Avenue penthouse would do it.

What was it with women? How could they say something at the start of an affair even when they damned well didn't mean it?

"I am completely dedicated to my career," Ingrid had said in that sexy Germanic purr of hers after the first time they'd gone to bed. "You need to know that, Rafe. I am not at all interested in settling down, so if you are—"

Him? Settle down? He still remembered how he'd laughed and rolled her beneath him. The perfect woman, he'd thought as he began making love to her again. Gorgeous. Sexy. Independent...

Yeah. Right.

His cell phone rang. He yanked it from his pocket, glared at the number on the screen and dumped the thing back into his jacket. It was Dante. The last thing he wanted was to talk to one of his brothers. The image in his head was still too fresh. Ingrid, opening the door. Ingrid, not wearing something slinky and sophisticated for their dinner reservations at Per Se but wearing, instead... What? An apron? Not the serviceable kind his mother wore but a thing that was all ruffles and lace and ribbons.

Ingrid, smelling not of Chanel but of roast chicken.

"Surprise," she'd trilled. "I'm making dinner tonight!"

She was? But she had no domestic skills. She'd told him that. Laughed about it.

Not tonight. Tonight she'd walked her fingers up his chest and whispered, "I'll bet you didn't know I could cook, *liebling*."

Except for the *liebling*, it was a line he'd heard before. It made his blood run cold.

The scene that played out next had been all too predictable, especially her shrill accusations that it was time to take their relationship to a new level and his blurting out, "What relationship?"

Rafe could still hear the sound of whatever it was she'd thrown at him hitting the door as he exited.

His cell phone rang again. And again, until finally he cursed, hauled the damned thing from his pocket and flipped it open.

"What?" he barked.

"And good evening to you, too, bro."

Rafe scowled. A woman walking toward him veered away.

"I am not in the mood for games, Dante. You got that?"

"Got it," his brother said cheerfully. Silence. Then Dante cleared his throat. "Problems with the Valkyrie?"

"Not a one."

"Good. Because I'd hate to lay this on you if you and she are—"

"Lay what on me?"

His brother's sigh came through the phone.

"Command performance, eight o'clock tomorrow morning. The old man wants to see us."

"I hope you told him what he can do with that request."

"Hey, I'm just the messenger. Besides, Mama called, not him."

"Hell. Is he supposed to be at death's door again? Did you tell her he's too mean to die?"

"No," Dante said reasonably. "Would you?"

It was Rafe's turn to sigh. They all adored their mother and sisters even though they seemed able to forgive Cesare Orsini anything. His sons could not. They'd figured out what their father was years ago.

"Damn it," Rafe said, "he's sixty-five, not ninety-five. He's got years ahead of him."

"Look, I don't want to listen to more endless speeches about where his banks are and what the combination is to his safe and the names of his lawyers and his accountants any more than you do. But could I tell that to Mama?"

Rafe's scowl deepened. "All right. Eight o'clock. I'll meet you guys there."

"It's just you and me, man. Nick's leaving for London tonight, remember? Falco heads for Athens in the morning."

"Terrific."

There was a brief silence. Then Dante said, "So, it's over with you and the Valkyrie?"

Rafe thought of saying everything from "No" to "What makes you think that?" Instead, he shrugged.

"She said it was time to reassess our relationship."

Dante offered a succinct, one-word comment. It made Rafe laugh; he could almost feel his black mood slipping away.

"I've got a cure for Relationship Reassessment," Dante said.

"Yeah?"

"I've got a date with that redhead in half an hour. Want me to call, see if she's got a friend?"

"I'm off women for a while."

"Yeah, yeah, I've heard that before. Well, if you're certain…"

"On the other hand, what is it they say about getting right back on a horse after you fall off?"

Dante laughed. "I'll call you back in ten."

Wrong. He called back in five. The redhead had a friend. And she'd be delighted to meet Rafe Orsini.

Well, hell, Rafe thought smugly as he hailed a cab, what woman wouldn't?

He overslept the next morning, showered quickly, skipped shaving, pulled on a black cotton sweater, faded jeans and sneakers and got to his parents' place before Dante.

Cesare and Sofia lived in a town house in Greenwich Village. Half a century ago, when Cesare had bought the house, the area had actually been part of Little Italy. Times had changed. The narrow streets had turned upscale and chic.

Cesare had changed, too. He'd gone from being a low-ranking mobster to being first a *capo*—the head of the syndicate—and then the boss. A *don*, though in Sicilian vernacular, the old Italian title of respect had a meaning all its own. Cesare owned a private sanitation company and half a dozen other legitimate businesses, but his true profession was one he would never confirm to his wife, his sons, his daughters.

Rafe went up the steps of the town house and rang the bell. He had a key but never used it. This place had not been his home for many years; he had not even thought of it as home long before he'd left it.

The house was enormous, especially by Manhattan standards. Cesare had used the increasingly large amounts of money brought in by his various enterprises to buy the houses on either side and convert the three buildings into one. Sofia presided over it all with no domestic help. A proper Sicilian housewife, she had always cooked and cleaned for her family. Rafe suspected it helped her cling to the fiction that her husband was just an everyday businessman.

Sofia greeted him as she always did, with a kiss on each cheek and a hug, as if she had not seen him in months instead of a couple of weeks. The she stepped back and gave him a critical look.

"You have not shaved this morning."

To his chagrin, Rafe felt himself blush. "Sorry, Mama. I wanted to be sure I got here on time."

"Sit," she commanded, as she led him into the vast kitchen. "Have breakfast."

The oak table was covered with bowls and platters. Telling her he'd already had the half grapefruit and black coffee that was his usual morning meal would have invited a lecture on nutrition, Orsini-style, so Rafe took a little of this, a little of that and put them on a plate. Dante sauntered in a couple of minutes later. Sofia kissed him, told him he needed a haircut and pointed him at the table.

"*Mangia,*" she commanded, and Dante, who took orders from no one, sheepishly complied.

The brothers were on their second espresso when Cesare's *capo*, a man who had served him for years, appeared.

"Your father will see you now."

The brothers put down their forks, patted their lips with their napkins and stood. Felipe shook his head.

"No, not together. One at a time. Raffaele, you are first."

Rafe and Dante looked at each other. "It's the prerogative of popes and kings," Rafe said with a tight smile, his words soft enough so they wouldn't reach the ears of Sofia, who was stirring a pot of sauce at the stove.

Dante grinned. "Have fun."

"Yeah. I'm sure it'll be a blast."

Cesare was in his study, a dark room made even darker by its overabundance of heavy furnishings, walls crowded with melancholy paintings of madonnas and saints and framed photographs of unknown relatives from the old country. Wine-colored drapes hung at the French doors and windows that overlooked the garden.

Cesare himself was seated behind his mahogany desk.

"Shut the door and wait outside," he told Felipe, and motioned Rafe to a chair. "Raffaele."

"Father."

"You are well?"

"I am fine," Rafe said coolly. "And you?"

Cesare seesawed his hand from side to side. "*Cosi cosa.* I am all right."

Rafe raised his eyebrows. "Well, that's a surprise." He slapped his hands on his thighs and rose to his feet. "In that case, since you're not at death's door—"

"Sit down."

Rafe's dark blue eyes deepened in color until they were almost black.

"I am not Felipe. I am not your wife. I am not anyone who takes orders from you, Father. I have not done so for many years."

"No. Not since the day you graduated from high school and told me you were going to a fancy university on a scholarship, and told me what I could do with your tuition money," Cesare said blandly. "Did you think I had forgotten?"

"You have your dates wrong," Rafe said, even more coldly. "I haven't taken orders from you since I discovered how you earned your money."

"So self-righteous," Cesare mocked. "You think you know everything, my son, but I promise you, any man can step into the darkness of passion."

"I don't know what in hell you're talking about and, frankly, I don't care. Goodbye, Father. I'll send Dante in."

"Raffaele. Sit down. This will not take long."

A muscle knotted in Rafe's jaw. Hell, why not? he thought. Whatever his father wanted to tell him this time might be amusing. He sat, stretched out his long legs, crossed them at the ankles and folded his arms over his chest.

"Well?"

Cesare hesitated. It was remarkable to see; Rafe couldn't recall ever seeing his father hesitant before.

"It is true," his old man finally said. "I am not dying."

Rafe snorted.

"What I wished to discuss with you that last time, I did not. I, ah, I was not prepared to do so, though I thought I was."

"A mystery," Rafe said, his tone making it

clear that nothing his father could say would be of interest.

Cesare ignored the sarcasm. "As I said, I am not dying." Another beat of hesitation. "But I will, someday. No one ever knows the exact moment but it is possible, as you know, that a man in my, ah, my profession can sometimes meet an unanticipated end."

Another first. Cesare had never made even token acknowledgment of his ties before.

"Is this your not-so-subtle way of telling me something's coming? That Mama, Anna and Isabella might be in danger?"

Cesare laughed. "You have seen one too many movies, Raffaele. No. Nothing is, as you put it, 'coming.' Even if it were, the code of our people forbids harming family members."

"They are *your* people," Rafe said sharply, "not 'ours.' And I am not impressed by honor among jackals."

"When my time comes, your mother, your sisters, you and your brothers will all be well taken care of. I am a wealthy man."

"I don't want any of your money. Neither do my brothers. And we are more than capable of taking good care of Mama and our sisters."

"Fine. Give the money away. It will be yours to do with as you wish."

Rafe nodded. "Great." He started to rise from his chair again. "I take it this conversation is—"

"Sit down," Cesare said, and then added the one word Rafe had never heard from him. "Please."

The head of the New York families sat forward. "I am not ashamed of the way I've lived," he said softly. "But I have done some things that perhaps I should not have done. Do you believe in God, Raffaele? Never mind answering. For myself, I am not certain. But only a foolish man would ignore the possibility that the actions of his life may one day affect the disposition of his soul."

Rafe's lips twisted in a cool smile. "Too late to worry about that."

"There are some things I did in my youth—" Cesare cleared his throat. "They were wrong. They were not done for the good of *la famiglia* but for me. They were selfish things and they have stained me."

"And this has what to do with me?"

Cesare's eyes met his son's. "I am asking you to help me put one of them right."

Rafe almost laughed. Of all the bizarre requests...

"I stole something of great value from a man who once helped me when no one else would," Cesare said gruffly. "I want to make amends."

"Send him a check," Rafe said with deliberate cruelty. What did all this have to do with him? His father's soul was his father's business.

"It is not enough."

"Make it a big check. Or, hell, make him an offer he can't refuse." Rafe's lips thinned. "That's you, isn't it? The man who can buy or intimidate his way into anything?"

"Raffaele. As a man, as your father, I am pleading for your help."

The plea was astounding. Rafe despised his father for who he was, what he was…but, unbidden, other memories rushed in. Cesare, pushing him on a swing at a playground. Cesare, soothing him when the clown hired for his fourth birthday party had scared him half to death.

His father's eyes burned with guilt. What would it take to hand-deliver a check and offer a long-overdue apology? Like it or not, this man had given life to him, his brothers and his sisters. He had, in his own manner, loved them and taken care of them. In some twisted way, he had even helped make them what they were. If he'd developed a conscience, even at this late date, wasn't that a good thing?

"Raffaele?"

Rafe took a deep breath. "Yeah. Okay." He spoke briskly because he knew how easy it would be to change his mind. "What do you want me to do?"

"I have your word that you will do it?"

"Yes."

Cesare nodded. "You will not regret this, I promise."

Ten minutes later, after a long, complex and yet oddly incomplete story, Rafe leaped to his feet.

"Are you insane?" he shouted.

"It is a simple request, Raffaele."

"Simple?" Rafe laughed. "That's a hell of a way to describe asking me to go to a godforsaken village in Sicily and marry some—some nameless, uneducated peasant girl!"

"She has a name. Chiara. Chiara Cordiano. And she is not a peasant. Her father, Freddo Cordiano, owns a vineyard. He owns olive groves. He is an important man in San Giuseppe."

Rafe leaned across his father's desk, slapped his hands on the brilliantly polished mahogany surface and glared.

"I am not marrying this girl. I am not marrying anyone. Is that clear?"

His father's gaze was steady. "What is clear is the value of the word of my firstborn son."

Rafe grabbed a handful of his father's shirt and hauled him to his feet. "Watch what you say to me," he snarled.

Cesare smiled. "Such a hot temper, my son. Much as you try to deny it, the Orsini blood beats in your veins."

Slowly Rafe let go of the shirt. He stood upright, drew a deep, steadying breath.

"I live by my word, Father. But you extracted it with a lie. You said you needed my help."

"And I do. You said you would give it to me. Now you say you will not." His father raised his eyebrows. "Which of us told the lie?"

Rafe stepped back. He counted silently to ten. Twice. Finally he nodded.

"I gave my word, so I'll go to Sicily and meet with this Freddo Cordiano. I'll tell him you regret whatever it was you did to him decades ago. But I will not marry his daughter. Are we clear about that?"

Cesare shrugged. "Whatever you say, Raffaele. I cannot force your compliance."

"No," Rafe said grimly. "You cannot."

He strode from the room, using the French doors that opened into the garden. He had no wish to see his mother or Dante or anyone.

Marriage? No way, especially not by command, especially not to suit his father—especially not to a girl born and raised in a place forgotten by time.

He was a lot of things, but he wasn't crazy.

More than four thousand miles away, in the rocky fortress that her father called his home and she called her prison, Chiara Cordiano shot to her feet in disbelief.

"You did what?" she said in perfect Florentine Italian. "You did *what*?"

Freddo Cordiano folded his arms over his chest. "When you speak to me, do so in the language of our people."

"Answer the question, Papa," Chiara said, in the rough dialect her father preferred.

"I said, I found you a husband."

"That's insane. You cannot marry me to a man I've never even seen."

"You forget yourself," her father growled. "That is what comes of all the foolish ideas put in your head by those fancy governesses your mother demanded I employ. I am your father. I can marry you to whomever I wish."

Chiara slapped her hands on her hips. "The son of one of your cronies? An American gangster? No. I will not do it, and you cannot make me."

Freddo smiled thinly. "Would you prefer that I lock you in your room and keep you there until you grow so old and ugly that no man wants you?"

She knew his threat was empty. He would not lock her in her room. Instead he would keep her a prisoner in this horrible little town, in these narrow, ancient streets she'd spent most of her twenty-four years praying to leave. She had tried leaving before. His men, polite but relentless, brought her back. They would do so again; she would never be free of a life she hated.

And he would surely not permit her to avoid marriage forever. She was a bargaining chip, a means of expanding or securing his vile empire.

Marriage.

Chiara suppressed a shudder.

She knew what that would be like, how men like her father treated their women, how he had treated her mother. This man, though American, would be no different. He would be cold. Cruel.

He would smell of garlic and cigars and sweat. She would be little more than his servant, and at night he would demand things of her in his bed...

Tears of anger glittered in Chiara's violet eyes. "Why are you doing this?"

"I know what is best for you. That is why."

That was a laugh. He never thought of her. This marriage was for his own purposes. But it wasn't going to take place. She was desperate, but she wasn't crazy.

"Well? Have you come to your senses? Are you prepared to be a dutiful daughter and do as you are told?"

"I'd sooner die," she said, and though she wanted to run, she forced herself to make a cool, stiff-backed exit. But once she'd reached the safety of her own room and locked the door behind her, she screamed in rage, picked up a vase and flung it at the wall.

Twenty minutes later, calmer, cooler, she splashed her face with water and went looking for the one man she loved. The man who loved her. The one man she could turn to.

"Bella mia," Enzo said, when she found him, "what is wrong?"

Chiara told him. His dark eyes grew even darker.

"I will save you, *cara*," he said.

Chiara threw herself into his arms and prayed that he would.

CHAPTER TWO

RAFE decided not to tell anyone where he was going.

His brothers would have laughed or groaned, and there were certainly no friends with whom he'd discuss the Machiavellian intrigues of the Orsini *don* and his interpretation of Sicilian honor.

Honor among thieves, Rafe thought grimly as his plane touched down at Palermo International Airport. He'd had to take a commercial flight; Falco had taken the Orsini plane to Athens. But even without the benefit of coming in via private jet, he moved swiftly through Passport Control.

Rafe's mood was dark. The only thing that kept him from snarling was knowing he'd have this ridiculous errand behind him in a day.

Maybe, he thought as he stepped out of the terminal into the heat of a Sicilian early autumn, just maybe he'd buy his brothers a round of drinks in a couple of weeks and when they were all laughing and relaxed he'd say, "You'll never guess where I was last month."

He'd tell them the story. All of it, starting with his meeting with Cesare. And they'd nod with approval when he described how gently he'd told Chiara Cordiano he was sorry but he wasn't about to marry her and, yes, he would be gentle because, after all, it wasn't the girl's fault.

A weight seemed to lift from his shoulders.

Okay. This might not be as bad as he'd figured. What the hell, this was a nice day for a drive. He'd have lunch at some picturesque little *trattoria* on the way to San Giuseppe, phone Freddo Cordiano and tell him he was en route. Once he arrived, he'd shake the old guy's gnarled hand, say something polite to the daughter and be back in Palermo by evening. His travel agent had booked him into a hotel that had once been a palace; she'd said it was elegant. He'd have a drink, then dinner on the balcony of his suite. Or maybe he'd stop at the bar. Italian women were among the most beautiful in the world. Well, not the one he was on his way to see, but she'd be history by evening.

By the time he reached the car rental counter, Rafe was smiling…

But not for long.

He'd reserved an SUV, or the Italian equivalent. Generally, he disliked SUVs—he preferred low, fast cars like the 'Vette he had back home, but he'd checked a map and San Giuseppe was high in the mountains. The road to it looked as if it might be more a goat track than anything else, so he'd opted for the traction of an SUV.

What waited at the curb was not an SUV. It was the one kind of car he actually despised, a big, black American thing, a model long favored by his father and his pals.

A Mobster Special.

The clerk shrugged and said there must have been a communications error but, *scusi*, this was all she had.

Perfect, Rafe thought as he got behind the wheel. A gangster's son on a gangster's errand, driving a gangster's car. All he needed was a fat cigar between his teeth.

So much for being in a better mood.

Things didn't improve after that. He'd been far too generous, calling the ribbon of potholed dirt with the steep slope of the mountain on one side and a dizzying plummet to the valley on the other a goat track.

It was more like a disaster waiting to happen.

Ten miles. Twenty. Thirty, and he'd yet to see another car. Not that he was complaining. There wasn't really enough room for two cars. There wasn't really enough room for—

Something black bolted from the trees and into the road.

Rafe cursed and stood on the brakes. The tires fought for purchase; the big car shimmied from side to side. It took all his skill to bring it to a stop. When he did, the hood was inches from the yawning space that overhung the valley.

He sat absolutely still. His hands, clutching the steering wheel, were trembling. He could hear the faint tick-tick of the cooling engine, the thud of his own heart.

Gradually the ticking of the engine faded. His heartbeat slowed. He dragged air into his lungs. Okay. The thing to do was back up, very carefully…

Something banged against his door. Rafe turned toward the half-open window. There was a guy outside the car and he was obviously dressed for an early Halloween. Black shirt. Black trousers. Black boots.

And an ancient, long-barreled black pistol, pointed straight at Rafe's head.

He'd heard stories of road bandits in Sicily and laughed them off, but only a jackass would laugh at this.

The guy made some kind of jerking motion with the pistol. What did it mean? Get out of the car? Hell, no. Rafe wasn't about to do that. The pistol waved again. Or was it shaking? Was the *guy* shaking? Yeah. He was, and that was not good. A nervous thief with a gun…

A nervous thief with white, wispy hair and rheumy eyes. And liver spots on the hand that held the pistol.

Wonderful. He was going to be robbed and killed by somebody's grandfather.

Rafe cleared his throat. "Easy, Grandpa," he said, even though the odds were good the old boy couldn't understand a word of English. He held up his hands, showed that they were empty, then slowly opened the door. The bandit stepped to the side and Rafe got out, carefully skirting the edge of the road and the void beyond it. "Do you speak English?" Nothing. He searched his memory. "*Voi*, ah, *voi parlate inglese*?" Still nothing. "Okay, look, I'm going to take my wallet from my pocket and give it to you. Then I'm gonna get back in the car and—"

The pistol arced through the air. He tried not to wince as it wobbled past his face.

"Watch yourself, Gramps, or that thing's liable to go off. Okay. Here comes my wallet—"

"No!"

The old man's voice shook. Shaking voice. Shaking hand. This was getting better and better. It would make an even better story than the one he'd already figured on telling his brothers, assuming he lived to tell it.

"Hugoahway!"

Hugoahway? What did that mean? The old guy's name, maybe, but it didn't sound Italian or Sicilian.

The old man poked the end of the pistol into Rafe's flat belly. Rafe narrowed his eyes.

Another poke. Another gruff "Hugoahway" and, damn it, enough was enough. Rafe grabbed the barrel of the pistol, yanked it from the bandit's shaking fingers and tossed it over the cliff.

"Okay," he said, reaching for the old man, "okay, that's— Oof!"

Something hit him, hard, from the rear. It was a second thief, wrapping his arms around Rafe's neck as he climbed on his back. Rafe grabbed his assailant's arms and wrenched the guy off him. The thief grunted, struggled, but he was a light-weight, and Rafe swung him around, worked his hands down to the guy's wrists…

Hell, this one was only a kid. Not just light-weight but flyweight. The kid, too, was dressed all in black, this time including a deep-brimmed, old-fashioned fedora that obscured his face.

A flyweight, but a fighter.

The kid was all over him, kicking, trying to claw him, damn it, trying to bite him! Rafe hoisted the boy to his toes.

"Stop it," he shouted.

The kid snarled something unintelligible in return, lifted a knee and took aim. Rafe twisted away.

"Are you deaf, boy? I said, stop!"

Evidently, *stop* didn't translate well because the kid didn't. He came at Rafe and the old guy joined the fracas, pummeling him with what looked like a small tree branch.

"Hey," Rafe said indignantly. This was not how things were supposed to go. He was the tough guy here; tough guys didn't get beaten up by boys and old men. He knew damned well he could stop the attack, just a couple of good punches would do it, but the thought of hitting Methuselah and a teenage delinquent was unappealing.

"Look," he said reasonably, "let's sort this out. Gramps, put down that stick. And you, boy, I'm gonna let go of you and—"

Bad move. The kid aimed his knee again. This time, he caught Rafe where he lived with devastating accuracy. Rafe grunted with pain, drew back his fist and managed a right cross to the kid's jaw.

It must have been a good one because the boy went down in a heap.

Still struggling for air, Rafe started to turn toward the old man. "Listen to me," he gasped....

The tree limb whacked him in the back of his head.

And Rafe went down beside the kid.

He came around slowly.

Ah, God, his head hurt. Methuselah had crowned him, the kid had kneed him. He had been totally and completely humiliated.

Could the day get any worse?

The old guy was sitting in the road, holding the kid in his arms, rocking him, talking to him in rapid and seemingly anguished Sicilian. He didn't even look up as Rafe rose painfully to his feet.

"Okay," he said gruffly, "okay, old man. Stand up. You hear me? Let go of the kid and get up."

The old man ignored him. Rafe reached down and grabbed a spindly arm. "I said, stand up!"

"Hugoahway!" the old guy shouted, and suddenly the words made sense. What he was saying was, *You go away.* Well, hell, he'd definitely oblige, but first he had to make sure the boy was okay. Stopping this unlikely duo from robbing him was one thing; killing them was another.

Rafe shoved the bandit aside, reached for the unconscious boy, lifted him into the crook of his arm. The kid moaned, his hat fell off, and...

And the boy wasn't a boy at all.

He was—*she* was a girl. No. Not a girl. A woman with a pale oval face and a silky mass of long, dark hair. He'd KO'd a woman. So much for wondering if the day could get any worse.

Carefully he scooped her up, ignored the old guy pulling at his sleeve and carried her to the side of the road that abutted the sloping mountain. Her head lolled back. He could see the pulse beating hard in the delicate hollow of her throat. The angle of her body made her breasts thrust against the rough wool of her jacket.

He set her down against the grassy rise. She was still unconscious.

She was also incredibly beautiful.

Only an SOB would notice such a thing at a moment like this, but only a fool would not. Her hair wasn't just dark, it was the color of a cloudless night. Her brows were delicate wings above her closed eyes; her lashes were dark shadows against razor-sharp cheekbones. Her nose was straight and narrow above a rosy-pink mouth.

Rafe felt a stir of lust low in his belly. And wasn't that terrific? Lust for a woman who'd tried to turn him into a eunuch, who'd played back-up to an old man with a pistol...

Who now lay helpless before him.

Damn it, he thought, and he caught the woman by the shoulders and shook her.

"Wake up," he said sharply. "Come on. Open your eyes."

Her lashes trembled, then slowly lifted, and he saw that her eyes were more than a match for the rest of her face, the irises not blue but the color of spring violets. Her lips parted; the tip of her tongue, delicate and pink, slicked across her mouth.

This time, the hunger that rolled through his belly made him sit back on his heels. Was this all it took? Was being on Sicilian soil enough to make him revert to the barbarian instincts of his ancestors?

Clarity was returning to her eyes. She put her hand to her jaw, winced, then shot him a look filled with hatred.

Those soft-looking pink lips drew back from small, perfect white teeth. *"Stronzo,"* she snarled.

It was a word any kid who'd grown up in a household where the adults often spoke in Italian would surely understand, and it made him laugh. Big mistake. She sat up, said it again and swung a fist at his jaw. He ducked it without effort and when she swung again, he caught her hand in his.

"That's a bad idea, baby."

She hissed through her teeth and shot a look over his shoulder at the old man.

Rafe shook his head.

"Another bad idea. You tell him to come at me, he'll get hurt." Disdain shone in her eyes. "Yeah, I know. You figure he got me the first time but, see, here's the thing. I don't get taken twice. You got that?"

A string of words flew from her lips. Rafe understood a couple of them but you didn't need a degree in Italian to get their meaning. The look in her eyes told him everything he needed to know.

"Yeah, well, I'm not a fan of yours, either. Is this how you and Gramps welcome visitors? You rob them? Hijack their cars? Maybe send them tumbling down into the valley?"

Her mouth curled, almost as if she'd understood him, but of course she hadn't. Not that it mattered. The question was, what did he do with this pair? Leave them here was his first instinct—but shouldn't he notify the authorities? Yes, but he'd heard stories about Sicily and the cops. For all he knew, this pair were the Italian equivalent of Robin Hood and Little John—except, Little John had turned out to be Maid Marian.

The woman had a faint mark on her jaw where he'd slugged her. He'd never hit a woman in his life and it bothered him. For all he knew, she needed medical care. He didn't think so, not from the way she was acting, but he felt some responsibility toward her, even if he'd only done what he had to do to protect himself.

He could just see telling that to a local judge: "Well, you see, sir, she came at me. And I hit her in self-defense."

It was the absolute truth but it would probably just give the locals a laugh. He was six foot three;

he weighed a tight 240 pounds. She was, what, five-six? And probably weighed 120 pounds less than he did.

Okay. He'd drive the duo home. Maybe what had happened had taught them a lesson.

Rafe cleared his throat. "Where do you and Gramps live?"

She stared at him, chin raised in defiance.

"Ah, *dove è—dove è* your house? Your *casa*?"

The woman jerked her hand free. She glared at him. He glared back.

"I'm willing to drive you and Grandpa home. You got that? No cops. No charges. Just don't push your luck."

She laughed. It was the kind of laugh that made Rafe's eyes narrow. Who in hell did she think she was? And what was there for her to laugh about? She'd come at him, yes, but she was the one who'd lost the fight. Now she was out here in the middle of nowhere, at the mercy of a man twice her size.

A man who was angry as hell.

It would take him less than a heartbeat to show her who was in charge, that she was at his mercy, that he had only to cup that perfect, beautiful face in his hands, put his mouth to hers and she'd stop looking at him with such disdain, such coldness, such rage.

A kiss, just one, and her mouth would soften. The rigidity of her muscles would give way to silken compliancy. Her lips would part, she'd loop her arms around his neck and whisper to him and he'd understand that whisper because a man and a woman didn't need to speak the same language to know desire, to turn anger to something hotter and wilder…

Rafe shot to his feet. "Stand up," he growled.

She didn't move. He gestured with his hand.

"I said, stand up. And you, old man, get in the back of the car."

The old man didn't move. Nobody did. Rafe leaned toward the woman.

"He's old," he said softly, "and I really have no desire to rough him up, so why don't you just tell him to do what I said."

She understood him. He could see it in her face.

Rafe shrugged. "Okay, we'll do it the hard way."

Her violet eyes flashed. She got to her feet, rattled off a string of words, and the old man nodded, walked to the car and climbed into the back.

Rafe jerked his thumb toward the car. "Now you."

One last glare. Then she turned away, marched to the car and started to climb in beside the old guy.

"The passenger seat," Rafe snapped. "Up front."

She said something. It was something women didn't say, not even on the streets of his youth.

"Anatomically impossible," he said coldly.

Color rose in her face. Good. She *did* understand English, at least a little. That would make things easier. She got into the car. He slammed the door after her, went around to the driver's side and climbed behind the wheel.

"How far up the mountain do you live?"

She folded her arms.

Rafe ground his teeth together, started the car, carefully backed away from the sheer drop and continued up the road in silence. Minutes passed, as did miles. And just when he'd pretty much given up hope he'd ever see civilization again, a town appeared. A wooden signpost that looked as if it had been here forever announced its name.

San Giuseppe.

He stopped the car and took in his first sight of the Sicily of his father.

Houses overhung a narrow, cobblestoned street

that wound its steep way up the mountain. Washing hung on clotheslines strung across rickety-looking balconies. The steeple of a church pierced a cloudless sky that overlooked a line of donkeys plodding after a small boy.

Cesare had insisted on showing him a couple of grainy snapshots of the town, taken more than fifty years ago. Nothing had changed, including the castle that loomed over it all.

Castello Cordiano.

Rafe put the car in gear. The woman beside him shook her head and reached for the door.

"You want to get out here?"

An arrogant lift of her chin brought into prominence the bruise he'd inflicted. Guilt racked him and he took a deep breath.

"Listen," he said. "About your jaw…"

Another flash of those violet eyes as she swung toward him.

"Yeah, I know. Believe me, the feeling's mutual. All I'm trying to say is that you should put some ice on that bruise. It'll keep the swelling down. And take some aspirin. You know what aspirin is? As-pi-rin," he said, knowing how idiotic he must sound but not knowing any other way to get his message through.

She snapped out an order. The old man replied; his tone suggested he was protesting but she repeated the order and he sighed, opened the door and stepped from the car.

Rafe caught her elbow as she moved to follow the old guy.

"Did you understand what I said? Ice. And aspirin. And—"

"I understood every word," she said coldly. "Now see if *you* understand, *signor*. Go away. Do you hear me? Go away, just as Enzo told you to do."

Rafe stared at her. "You speak English?"

"I speak English. And Italian, and the Sicilian form of it. You, quite obviously, do not." Those stunning eyes narrowed until only a slash of color showed. "You are not welcome here. And if you do not leave of your own accord, Enzo will see to it that you do."

"Enzo? You mean Grandpa?" Rafe laughed. "That's one hell of a threat, baby."

"He is more a man than you will ever be."

"Is he," Rafe said, his voice gone low and dangerous and instead of thinking, he caught her by the shoulders and lifted her across the console, into his lap. She struggled, beat at him with her fists but he was ready. He caught both her hands in one of his, slid the other into her hair, tilted her head back and kissed her.

Kissed her as he'd fantasized kissing her, back on that road. She fought, but it was pointless. He was hot with fury and humiliation…

Hot with the feel of her against him. Her mouth, soft under his. Her breasts, tantalizing against the hardness of his chest. Her rounded backside, digging into in his lap.

His body reacted in a heartbeat, his sex swelling until he was sure it had never been this huge or throbbed with such urgency. She felt it happen; how could she not? He heard her little cry of shock, felt it whisper against his mouth. Her lips parted and she tried to bite him but he turned the attempt against her, used it as a chance to deepen the kiss, to slip his tongue into the silky warmth of her mouth. She gasped again, made a little sound of distress…

And then something happened.

Her mouth softened under his. Sweetened. Turned warm and willing, and the knowledge that he could take her, right here, right now, made his already-hard body turn to stone. He let go of her wrists, slid his hand under her jacket, cupped the delicate weight of her breast…

Her teeth sank into his lip.

Rafe jerked back and put his hand to the tiny wound. His finger came away bearing a drop of crimson.

"Pig," she said, her voice shaking. "No good, filthy pig!"

He stared at her, saw her shocked eyes, her trembling mouth, and heard his father's voice reminding him that any man could step into the darkness of overwhelming passion.

"Listen," he said, "listen, I didn't mean—"

She opened the door and bolted from the car, but not before she'd flung a string of Sicilian curses at him.

Hell, he thought, taking his handkerchief from his pocket and dabbing it against his lip, for all he knew, he deserved them.

CHAPTER THREE

WAS the American going to come after her?

Chiara ran blindly into the narrow alley that led to a long-forgotten entrance to Castello Cordiano, following its twists and turns as it climbed steeply uphill.

No one knew this passageway existed. She'd discovered it when she was a little girl, hiding in the nursery closet with her favorite doll to get away from her father's callousness and her mother's piety.

It had been her route to freedom ever since, and there was the added pleasure of fooling her father's men when she seemed to vanish from right under their noses.

The alley ended in a field of craggy stone outcroppings and brambles. A thick growth of ivy and scrub hid the centuries-old wooden door that led into the castle. Panting, hand to her heart, Chiara fell back against it and fought to catch her breath. She waited, then peered through a break in the tangled greenery. *Grazie Dio!* The American had not followed her.

Behaving like the brute he was must have satisfied him.

No surprise there. She'd always known how the world went. Men were gods. Women were their handmaids. The American had gone out of his way to remind her of those truths in the most basic way possible.

Chiara took a last steadying breath, opened the heavy door and slipped past it. A narrow corridor led to a circular staircase that wound into a gloomy darkness broken by what little light came through the *balistraria* set into the old stone walls. Long moments later, she emerged in the nursery closet. Carefully she stepped into the room itself, eased open the door, checked the corridor, then hurried halfway down its length to her bedroom.

Her heartbeat didn't return to normal until she was safely inside with the door shut behind her.

What a disaster this day had been!

Yes, she'd gotten farther from the castle than ever before, but so what? The plan to frighten the American and send him running had been a miserable failure. Worse than a failure because instead of frightening him, she'd infuriated him.

Angering a man like that was never a good idea.

Chiara touched the tip of her finger to her lip. Was his blood on her? It was not but she could still feel the imprint of his mouth, could still taste him. The warm, firm flesh. The quick slide of his tongue. The terrifying sense of invasion…

And then, without warning, that sensation low in her belly. As if something were slowly pulsing deep inside.

She blinked, dragged air into her lungs. Never mind going over what had happened. What mattered was what would happen next.

She had badly underestimated the American.

Where was the short, stocky, cigar-chomping pig she'd envisioned? Not that he wasn't a pig. He was, absolutely. The difference was that she could not have walked into a room and picked him out as one of the goons who did the work of men like her father.

He was too tall. Too leanly built. But it was more than looks that separated him from the men she knew. It was… What? His clothes? The gray, pinstriped suit that had surely been custom-made? The gold Rolex she'd glimpsed on his tanned, hair-dusted wrist?

Maybe it was his air of sophistication.

Or his self-assurance.

Smug self-assurance, even when Enzo had pointed a pistol at him. Even when she'd flung herself on his back. Even when she'd sunk her teeth into his lip to end that vile stamp of I'm-in-charge-here male domination.

That hot, possessive kiss.

Chiara jerked away from the door. She had to work quickly. *Dio*, if her father saw her now…

She almost laughed as she stripped off the ancient black suit and white, collarless shirt Enzo had found for her. Thinking about Enzo was enough to stop her laughter. What humiliation he had suffered today. And if her father ever learned what he had done…

He would pay a terrible price, and all because of her. She should not have run to him for help, but who else was there to turn to?

Enzo had listened to her story. Then he'd taken her hand in his.

"I can scare him off," he'd said. "Remember, he is not truly Sicilian. He is American, not one of us, and they are not the same. They are weak.

You will see, child. We will catch him by surprise. And while he is still immobilized, I will show him my pistol and tell him to go away. And he will be gone."

When she protested that it was too dangerous, Enzo had suddenly looked fierce and said he had done things of this sort in the past.

It was hard to imagine.

The old man was her dearest friend. Her only friend. He'd been her father's driver when she was little and he'd been kind to her, kinder than anyone, even her mother, but her mother had not been made for this world. Chiara had only vague memories of her, a thin figure in black, always kneeling in the old chapel or sitting in a straight-backed parlor chair bent over her Bible, never speaking, not even to Chiara, except to whisper warnings about what life held in store.

About men, and what they all wanted.

"Men are animals, *mia figlia*," she'd hissed. "They want only two things. Power over others. And to perform acts of depravity upon a woman's body."

Chiara kicked the telltale clothing into the back of her closet, then hurried into the old-fashioned bathroom and turned on the taps over the bathtub.

What her mother had told her was the truth.

Her father ruled his men and his town with an iron fist. As for the rest…she'd overheard the coarse jokes of his men. She'd felt their eyes sliding over her. One in particular looked at her in a way that made her feel ill.

Giglio, her father's second in command. He was an enormous blob of flesh. He had wet-looking red lips and his face was always sweaty. But it was his eyes that made her shudder. They were small. Close set. Filled with malice, like the eyes of a wild boar that had once confronted her on the mountain.

Giglio had taken to watching her with a boldness that was terrifying.

The other day, walking past her, his hand had brushed her buttocks and seemed to linger. She had gasped and shrunk from him; her father had been in the room. Hadn't he seen what had happened? Then why hadn't he reacted?

Chiara blanked her mind to the memory as she sank deep into the tub of hot water. She had more important things to worry about right now.

She and Enzo had failed. The American would keep his appointment with her father. The question was, would he recognize her? Enzo could keep out of his way but she couldn't. She was, after all, the reason for the American's visit.

She was on display. For sale, like a prize goat.

All she could do was pray that he would not recognize her. It was possible, wasn't it? She'd be wearing a dress, her hair would be scraped back into its usual bun, she would speak softly, behave demurely and keep her eyes on the floor. She would make herself as invisible as possible.

And even if he recognized her, she could only pray that he would not want her, even though it would be an honor for him to wed the daughter of Don Freddo Cordiano.

A man like that would surely refuse such a so-called honor. Why take her when he could have his pick of women? Though she found all that overt masculinity disgusting, she knew there were those who'd be dazzled by the rugged face, the piercing blue eyes, the hard, powerful body.

Dio, so powerful!

Heat suffused her cheeks.

That moment, when he'd pulled her onto his lap, when she'd felt him beneath her. The memory made her tremble. She had never imagined…

She knew a man's sexual organ had that ability. She was not ignorant. But that part of him had felt enormous. Surely a woman's body could not accommodate something of such size…

A knock sounded at the door. Chiara shot up straight in the water.

"*Sì?*"

"*Signorina, per favore, il vostro padre chiede che lo unite nella biblioteca.*"

Chiara held herself very still. Her father wanted her in the library. Was he alone, or had the American arrived? "*Maria? È solo, il mio padre?*"

"*No, signorina. Ci è un uomo con lui. Uno Americano. Ed anche il suo capo, naturelmente.*"

Oh God. Chiara closed her eyes. Not just the American. Giglio was there, too.

Could the day get any worse?

Could the day get any worse?

Rafe felt a muscle jump in his cheek. Why bother wondering? It already had.

First the nonsense with Robin Hood and Maid Marian. Then the girl sinking her teeth into his lip. Now this. Twenty minutes of being trapped in an uncomfortable chair in a library even more depressing than his father's, with a similar clutch of saints and stiffly posed ancestors looking down from the walls. He had an unwanted glass of *grappa* in his hand, a fat cigar he'd declined on the table beside him and the finishing touch, a butt-ugly mass of muscle and fat named Giglio, overflowing in a chair across from his.

Cordiano had introduced the man as a business associate. His *capo*, was more like it. It was the accessory *du jour* for hoodlums.

The *capo* had not taken his eyes off Rafe, and nasty eyes they were. Small. Set too close together. Unblinking and altogether mean. At first Rafe had ignored it, but it was getting to him.

For some reason the pig man didn't like him. Fine. The feeling was mutual.

Added to all that, Cordiano seemed intent on spinning endless, self-aggrandizing tales set in the glory days of his youth, when men were men and there was nothing anybody could do about it.

Rafe didn't care. All he wanted was to get out of here, back to Palermo, back to the States and a world that made sense, but until they got down to basics, he was stuck.

His attempts to move things along had gotten nowhere.

After the handshakes, the how-was-your-trip question and his it-was-fine response—because no way was he going to tell this sly old fox and his *capo* that he'd been had by a doddering old highwayman and a woman—after all that plus the ceremonial handing over of the unwanted cigar and the obligatory glass of *grappa*, Rafe had handed Cordiano his father's sealed letter.

"Grazie," the *don* said and tossed it, unopened, on his desk. Each time he paused for breath, Rafe tried to launch into the verbal form of his father's apology. No luck. Cordiano didn't give him a chance.

At least the marriage proposal had not been mentioned. Maybe Cesare had already explained that Rafe would not be availing himself of the generous offer to take his old enemy's obviously undesirable daughter off his hands.

Something must have shown in his face because the pig man's eyes narrowed. Rafe narrowed his in return. He felt foolish, like a kid doing his best to stare down the class bully, but what else did he have to keep him occupied?

"—for you, Signor Orsini."

Rafe blinked and turned toward Cordiano. "Sorry?"

"I said, this has surely been a long day for you and here I am, boring you with my stories."

"You're not boring me at all," Rafe said, and forced a smile.

"Is the *grappa* not to your liking?"

"I'm afraid I'm not a *grappa* man, Don Cordiano."

"And not a cigar man, either," Cordiano said, with a quick flash of teeth.

"Actually…" Rafe put his glass on the small table beside the chair and rose to his feet. The pig man stood up, too. Enough, Rafe thought. "I am also not a man who enjoys being watched as if I might steal the silver, so tell your watchdog to relax."

"Of course." The *don* chuckled, though the sound was remarkably cheerless. "It is only that Giglio sees you as competition."

"Trust me, Cordiano, I'm not the least bit interested in taking his job."

"No, no, certainly not. I only meant that he is aware that I have been searching for a way to thank him for his years of dedication, and—"

"And I'm sure you'll find an appropriate reward but that doesn't concern me. I'm here on behalf of my father. I'd appreciate it if you'd read his letter."

Cordiano smiled. "But I know what it says,

signor. Cesare begs my forgiveness for what he did almost half a century ago. And you, Raffaele—may I call you that?—and you are to assure me that he means every word. Yes?"

"That's pretty much it." And still not a word about daughters and marriage, thank God. "So, I can return home and tell him his apology is accepted? Because it's getting late. And—"

"Did your father tell you what it is he did?"

"No. He didn't. But that's between you and—"

"I was his—I suppose you would call it his sponsor."

"How nice for you both."

"He repaid my generosity by stealing *la mia fidanzata*."

"I'm sorry but I don't speak—"

"Your father stole my fiancée." Cordiano's smile turned cold. "He eloped with her in the middle of the night, two days before we were to marry."

"I don't understand. My father has a wife. She…" Rafe's jaw dropped. "Are you saying my mother was engaged to you?"

"Indeed she was, until your father stole her."

All that "dark passion" stuff was starting to make sense. Now what? What could he say? It was hard enough to picture a young Cesare but to imagine his mother as a young woman running away with him…

"Did you think this was about something simple?" The *don*'s voice was as frigid as his smile. "That is why he sent you here, boy. To offer a meaningful apology, one I would accept. An eye for an eye. That is our way."

Rafe shot a quick look at the *capo*. Was that what this was all about? He'd put in his time in the Marines; he and his brothers had all served their country. He could give a good account of himself against, what, 350 pounds of fat and muscle, but in the end…

"An eye for an eye. Or, now that so many years have gone by, a deed for a misdeed." Cordiano folded his arms over his chest. "Your father took my bride. I will show him forgiveness by letting you take my daughter as yours. Do you see?"

Did he see? Rafe almost laughed. No way. Not even a genius would see any logic in that.

"What I see," he said flatly, "is that you have a daughter you want to get rid of."

Pig Man made a humming sound deep in his throat.

"And somehow, you and my old man cooked

up this cockeyed scheme. Well, forget about it. It's not going to happen."

"My daughter needs a husband."

"I'm sure she does. Buy one, if that's what it takes."

The mountain of muscle grunted and took a step forward. Rafe could feel the adrenaline pumping. Hell, he thought, eyeing the *capo*, he could do more than put up a good fight. Angry as he was, he could take him.

"I have your father's word in this matter, Orsini."

"Then you have nothing, because it is not his word you need, it's mine. And I can damned well assure you that—"

"There you are," Cordiano said sharply, glaring past him. "It took you long enough to obey my orders, girl."

Rafe swung around. There was a figure in the doorway. Chiara Cordiano had come to join them. A weak finger of late-afternoon sunlight pierced a narrow gap in the heavy window draperies, lending a faint outline to her thin shape.

"Have you turned to stone?" the *don* snapped. "Step inside. There is a man here who wants to meet you."

Like hell he did, Rafe almost said, but he

reminded himself that none of this was the girl's fault. If anything, he felt a stab of pity for her. He'd already figured that she was homely. Maybe it was worse than that. For all he knew, she had warts the size of watermelons.

She was also a woman defeated. Everything about her said so.

She moved slowly. Her head was bowed, showing dark hair pulled back in a tight bun. Her hands were folded before her, resting at her waistline, assuming she had one. It was impossible to tell because her dress was shapeless, as black and ugly as her shoes. Lace-ups, he thought with incredulity, the kind he'd seen little old ladies wearing back home on Mulberry Street.

He couldn't see her face but he didn't need to. It would be as plain as the rest of her.

No wonder her father was trying to give her away. No man in his right mind would want such a pitiful woman in his bed.

Okay. He'd be polite. He could do that much, he thought, and opened his mouth to say hello.

Pig Man beat him to it.

"Buon giorno, signorina," the *capo* said.

Except, he didn't say it, he slimed it. How else

to describe the oiliness in the man's voice? Maybe Chiara Cordiano thought so, too. Rafe saw a tremor go through her narrow shoulders.

"Signor Giglio has spoken to you," the *don* snapped. "Where are your manners?"

"Buon giorno," she said softly.

Rafe cocked his head. Was there something familiar about her voice?

"And you have not greeted our guest, Signor Raffaele Orsini."

The woman inclined her head. Not easy to do; her chin was damned near already on her chest.

"Buon giorno," she whispered.

"In English, girl."

Her hands twisted together. Rafe felt another tug of sympathy. The poor thing was terrified.

"That's okay," he said quickly. "I don't know much Italian but I can manage a hello. *Buon giorno, signorina. Come sta?"*

"Answer him," Cordiano barked.

"I am fine, thank you, *signor."*

There was definitely something about her voice…

"Why are you dressed like this?" her father demanded. "You are not going into a convent. You are going to be married."

"Don Cordiano," Rafe said quickly, "I've already told you—"

"And why do you stand there with your head bowed?" Cordiano grabbed his daughter's arm, his fingers pressing hard. She winced, and Rafe took a step forward.

"Don't," he said quietly.

The *capo* lunged forward but Cordiano held up his hand.

"No, Giglio. Signor Orsini is correct. He is in charge of things now. It is his right, and his alone, to discipline his fiancée."

"She is not my…" Rafe shot the woman a quick glance, then lowered his voice. "I already told you, I am not interested in marrying your daughter."

Cordiano's eyes turned hard. "Is that your final word, Orsini?"

"What kind of man are you, to put your daughter through something like this?" Rafe said angrily.

"I asked you a question. Is that your final word?"

Could a man feel any worse than Rafe felt now? He hated what Cordiano was doing to the girl. Why in hell didn't she say something? Was she meek, or was she stupid?

Not my worry, he told himself, and looked at Freddo Cordiano.

"Yes," he said gruffly, "it is my final word."

Pig Man laughed. The *don* shrugged. Then he clamped his fingers around his daughter's delicate-looking wrist.

"In that case," he said, "I give my daughter's hand to my faithful second in command, Antonio Giglio."

At last the woman's head came up. "No," she whispered. "No," she said again, and the cry grew, gained strength, until she was shrieking it. "No! No! No!"

Rafe stared at her. No wonder she'd sounded familiar. Those wide, violet eyes. The small, straight nose. The sculpted cheekbones, the lush, rosy mouth…

"Wait a minute," he said, "just wait one damned minute…"

Chiara swung toward him. The American knew. Not that it mattered. She was trapped. Trapped! She had to do something…

Desperate, she wrenched her hand out of her father's.

"I will tell you the truth, Papa. You cannot give me to Giglio. You see—you see, the American and I have already met."

"You're damned right we have," Rafe said furiously. "On the road coming here. Your daughter stepped out of the trees and—"

"I only meant to greet him. As a gesture of—of goodwill." She swallowed hard; her eyes met Rafe's and a long-forgotten memory swept through him of being caught in a firefight in some miserable hellhole of a country when a terrified cat, eyes wild with fear, had suddenly, inexplicably run into the middle of it. "But...but he...he took advantage."

Rafe strode toward her. "Try telling your old man what really happened!"

"What *really* happened," she said in a shaky whisper, "is that—is that right there, in his car—right there, Papa, Signor Orsini tried to seduce me!"

Giglio cursed. Don Cordiano roared. Rafe would have said, "You're crazy, all of you," but Chiara Cordiano's dark lashes fluttered and she fainted, straight into his arms.

CHAPTER FOUR

IT WAS like being trapped in a nightmare. One minute, Rafe was about to launch into his father's all-too-florid verbal apology. The next—

The next, Chiara Cordiano was lying as limp as laundry in his arms.

Was she faking it? The woman was a class-A actress. First a tough bandit, then a demure *Siciliana*, when the truth was, she was anything but demure.

A little while ago, she'd attacked him with the ferocity of a lioness.

And there'd been that sizzling flash of sexual heat.

Oh, yeah. The lady was one hell of an actress and this was her best performance yet. Claiming he'd tried to seduce her. He'd kissed her, was all, and one kiss did not a seduction make.

The *don* was holding his *capo* back with a hand on his arm and an assortment of barked commands. Rafe knew that Pig Man wanted to kill him. Good. Let him try. He was more than in the mood to take on the load of lard.

First, though, the woman in his arms had to open her eyes and admit she'd lied.

He looked around, strode to a brocade-covered sofa and unceremoniously dumped her on it. "Chiara," he said sharply. No response. "Chiara," he said again, and shook her.

Pig Man snarled an obscenity. Rafe looked up.

"Get him out of here, Cordiano, or so help me, I'm gonna lay him out."

The *don* snapped out an order, pointed a finger at the door. The *capo* shrugged off his boss's hand. Like any well-trained attack dog, he did as he'd been ordered but not without one last threatening look at Rafe.

"This is not over, American."

Rafe showed his teeth in a grin. "Anytime."

The door swung shut. Cordiano went to a mahogany cabinet, poured brandy into a chunky crystal glass and held it out. Give it to her yourself, Rafe felt like saying but he took the glass, slipped an arm around Chiara's shoulders, lifted her up and touched the rim of the glass to her lips.

"Drink."

She gave a soft moan. Thick, dark lashes fluttered and cast shadows against her creamy skin. Wisps of hair had escaped the ugly bun and lay against her cheeks, as delicately curled as the interior of the tiny shells that sometimes washed up on the beach at Rafe's summer place on Nantucket Island.

She looked almost unbelievably fragile.

But she wasn't, he reminded himself. She was as tough as nails and as wily as a fox.

"Come on," he said sharply. "Open your eyes and drink."

Her lashes fluttered again, then lifted. She stared up at him, her pupils deep as a moonless night and rimmed by a border of pale violet.

"What…what happened?"

Nice. Trite, but nice.

"You passed out." He smiled coldly. "And right on cue."

Did defiance flash in those extraordinary eyes? He couldn't be sure; she leaned forward, laid cool, pale fingers over his tanned ones as she put her mouth to the glass.

Her throat worked as she swallowed. A couple of sips and then she looked up at him. Her lips glistened; her eyes were wide. The tip of her tongue swept over her lips and he could imagine those lips parted, that tongue tip extended, those eyes locked, hot and deep, on his—

A shot of raw lust rolled through him. He turned away quickly, put the glass on a table and stepped back.

"Now that you're among the living again, how about telling your old man the truth?"

"The truth about..." Her puzzled gaze went from her father to Rafe. "Oh!" she whispered, and her face turned scarlet.

Rafe's eyes narrowed. Her reactions couldn't be real. Not the Victorian swoon, not her behavior at the memory of what had happened in the car. He'd kissed her, for God's sake. That was it. He'd lifted her into his lap and kissed her and, okay, she'd ended up biting him, but only after she'd responded, after he'd gotten hard as stone and she'd felt it and...

And he'd behaved like an idiot.

He was not a man who did things like that to women. A little playing around during sex was one thing; he'd had lovers who liked a hint of domination, but having a woman whisper "more" even as she pretended something else was not the same as what had happened with Chiara Cordiano.

What in hell had gotten into him? He'd been furious, but anger had nothing to do with sex… did it?

It was a subject to consider at another time. Right now he might just have a problem on his hands. This culture had its roots in times long gone. Its rules, its mores, were stringent.

Back home, a kiss, even a stolen one, was just a kiss. Here it could be construed as something else.

"Don Cordiano," he said carefully, "I kissed your daughter. I'm sorry if I offended her."

"And I am to accept your apology?"

The *don*'s tone was arrogant. It made Rafe bristle.

"I'm not asking *you* to accept it," he said sharply, and turned to Chiara. "I shouldn't have kissed you. If I frightened you, I'm sorry."

"Perhaps you would care to explain how you managed to meet with my daughter before you met with me."

Perhaps he would, Rafe thought, but he'd be damned if he'd stand here and admit he'd almost been bested by a slip of a girl and an old man. Besides, that part of the story belonged to Cordiano's daughter, he thought grimly, and looked at her again. But she locked her hands together in her lap, bent her head and studied them as if she had no part in this conversation.

The hell with that.

"Your turn, *signorina*," Rafe said coldly.

Chiara felt her heart thump. The American was right.

This was the time for her to say, "You have it wrong, Papa. This man didn't 'meet' me, not the way you make it sound. I stopped him on the road and tried to scare him away."

What a joke!

Instead of scaring him away, she'd brought him straight to San Giuseppe. And she couldn't explain that, not without telling her father everything, and that meant she'd have to tell him about Enzo.

No matter what the consequences, exposing Enzo's part in the mess would be fatal.

She knew her father well. He would banish Enzo from San Giuseppe, the place where the old man had spent his entire life. Or—her heart banged into her throat—or Enzo could suffer an unfortunate accident, a phrase she'd heard her father use in the past.

She was not supposed to know such things, but she did. When she was little, her father would say that Gio or Aldo or Emilio had left his employ but by the time she was twelve, she'd figured it out.

No one "left" the *don*. They had accidents or vanished, and their names were never mentioned again.

She could not risk having such a thing happen to Enzo. And yet if she didn't come up with something, who knew what her father might do to Rafe Orsini? Not that she cared about him, but she surely didn't want *his* "accident" on her conscience.

"Well? I am waiting."

Her father wasn't talking to her; he was glaring at Raffaele Orsini…but she would reply. She would make up the story as she went along and pray the American would not correct her version.

"Papa. Signor Orsini and I met when I—when I—"

"Silence!" her father roared. "This does not concern you. Signor Orsini? I demand an explanation."

"Demand?" Rafe said softly.

"Indeed. I am waiting for you to explain your actions."

Her father's face was like stone. Chiara had seen men cower from that face. Orsini, for all his studied toughness, surely would do the same.

That patina of arrogant masculinity would crumble and he'd tell her father the entire story.

"I don't explain myself to anyone," the American said coldly.

Her father stiffened. "You came here to beg my forgiveness for an insult half a century old. Instead, you insult me all over again."

"I don't beg, either. I offered you my father's apology, and I apologized to your daughter. As far as I'm concerned, that ends our business."

Chiara held her breath. The room seemed locked in stillness, and then her father's lips curved in what was supposed to be a smile. But it was not; she knew it.

Still, what he said next surprised her.

"Very well. You are free to leave."

The American nodded. He started for the door as her father strode toward her.

"On your feet," he snarled.

Raffaele Orsini had already opened the door, but he paused and turned around at her father's words.

"Let's be clear about something, Cordiano. What happened—that I kissed your daughter— wasn't her fault."

"What you say has no meaning here. Now, get out. Chiara. Stand up."

Chiara rose slowly to her feet. Her father's face was a study in fury. She knew he would have hurt her if she were a man, but some old-world sense of morality had always kept him from striking her.

Still, he would not let what had happened pass. Raffaele Orsini could insist that the kiss had not been her fault until the end of eternity. Her father would never agree. A woman was supposed to defend her honor to her last breath.

She had not.

Someone had to pay for the supposed insult her father had suffered and who else could that someone be, if not her?

Her father's eyes fixed on hers. "Giglio!" he barked.

The *capo* must have been waiting just outside. He stepped quickly into the room.

"Si, Don Cordiano?"

"Did you hear everything?"

The fat man hesitated, then shrugged. *"Sì.* I heard."

"Then you know that my daughter has lost her honor."

Rafe raised his eyebrows. "Now, wait a damned minute…"

"All these years, I raised her with care."

"You didn't raise me at all," Chiara said, her voice trembling. "Nannies. Governesses—"

Her father ignored her. "I saw to it that she remained virtuous and saved her chastity for the marriage bed."

"Papa. What are you talking about? I have not lost my chastity! It was only a kiss!"

"Today, she chose to throw away her innocence." The *don*'s mouth twisted. "Such dishonor to bring on my home!"

Chiara laughed wildly. Rafe looked at her. Her cheeks were crimson; her eyes were enormous. Somehow the tight bun had come undone and her hair, thick and lustrous, swung against her shoulders.

"*I've* brought dishonor to this house?"

The *don* ignored her. His attention was on his *capo*.

"Giglio," he said, "my old friend. What shall I do?"

"Wait a minute," Rafe said, starting toward the *don*. Pig Man stepped in his path; he brushed him aside as if he were no more than a fly. "Listen to me, Cordiano. You're making this into something that never happened. I kissed your daughter. I sure as hell didn't take her virginity!"

"This is not America, Orsini. Our daughters do not flaunt their bodies. They do not let themselves be touched by strangers. And I am not talking to you. I am talking to *you*, Giglio, not to this…this *straniero*."

Pig Man said nothing, but his tiny eyes glittered.

"I cannot even blame him for what happened," Cordiano continued. "Foreigners know nothing of our ways. It was all my daughter's fault, Giglio, and now, what am I to do to restore our family's honor?"

Holy hell, Rafe thought, this was like something out of a really bad movie. The furious villain. The terrified virgin. And the pig, licking his thick lips and looking from the woman to the *don* as if the answer to the question might appear in neon in the space between them.

"Okay," Rafe said quickly, "okay, Cordiano, tell me what will stop this nonsense. You want me to direct my apology to you? Consider it done. What happened was my fault entirely. I regret it. I didn't mean to offend your daughter or you. There. Are you satisfied? I hope to hell you are because this…this farce has gone far enough."

He might as well have said nothing. Cordiano didn't even look at him. Instead, he spread his arms beseechingly at his *capo*.

Giglio was sweating. And all at once Rafe knew where this nightmare was heading.

"Wait a minute," he said, but Cordiano put his hand in the small of Chiara's back and sent her flying into the meaty arms of his *capo*.

"She is yours," he said in tones of disgust. "Just get her out of my sight."

"No!" Chiara's cry echoed in the room. "No! Papa, you cannot do this!"

She was right, Rafe thought frantically. Of course Cordiano couldn't do this. He wouldn't.

But Cordiano had taken a telephone from his desk. It, at least, was a symbol of modernity, bright and shiny and bristling with buttons. He pushed one, then spoke. Rafe's Italian was bad, his Sicilian worse, but he didn't need a translator to understand what he was saying.

He was arranging for Chiara and Pig Man to be married.

Chiara, who understood every word, went white. "Papa. Please, please, I beg you—"

Enough, Rafe thought, He tore the phone from Cordiano's hand and hurled it across the room.

"It's not going to happen," he growled.

"You are nobody here, Signor Orsini."

Rafe's lips stretched in a cold grin. "That's where you're wrong. I am always somebody. It's time you understood that. Chiara! Step away from the pig and come to me."

She didn't move. Rafe took his eyes from Cordiano long enough to steal a look at her. He cursed under his breath. That last faint had probably been a fake. This one wouldn't be. She wasn't just pale, she was the color of paper.

"Giglio. Let go of the lady."

Nothing. Rafe took a breath and dug his hand into his pocket, snagged his BlackBerry and shoved it forward so it made a telltale bulge. As he'd hoped, the *capo*'s eyes followed.

"Do it," he said through his teeth, "and you might have an unfortunate accident."

That was all it took. The pig's arms dropped to his sides. Despite everything, or maybe because of it, Rafe struggled not to laugh. He could almost hear his brothers' howls when he told them how he'd faked out a man who was surely a stone-cold killer with his trusty PDA.

"Chiara. Get over here."

She crossed the room slowly, her eyes never

leaving his. When she reached him, he took her wrist, brought her close to his side. She was shaking like a young tree in a wind storm; her skin felt clammy under his fingers. He cursed, slid his arm around her waist and tucked her against him. She came willingly and his anger toward her gave way to compassion. Sure, this whole damned mess was her fault—he'd kissed her, but if she hadn't pulled that stupid trick on the road, it never would have happened—but her father's reaction, even for an old-line Sicilian, was way out of line.

"It's okay," he said softly.

She nodded. Still, he could hear her teeth chattering.

"It's okay," he said again. "Everything's going to be fine."

She looked up at him, eyes glittering with unshed tears, and shook her head. Her loosened hair drifted across one side of her face and he fought back the sudden crazy desire to tuck the strands back behind her ear.

"No," she said, so softly that he could hardly hear her. "My father will give me to Giglio."

Rafe felt his muscles tense. Give her away. As if she were Cordiano's property.

"He won't. I won't let him."

Her mouth trembled. She said something, so quietly he couldn't hear it, and he cupped her face, lifted it to his.

"What did you say?"

She shook her head again.

"Chiara. Tell me what you said."

She took a long, deep breath, so deep that he could see the lift of her breasts even within the shapeless black dress.

"I said he will do what he wishes, Signor Orsini, once you have gone."

Was she right? Was this only a temporary respite from her father's crazed insistence that the only way to restore the honor she had not lost was by marrying her off?

The sound of slow applause made him look up. Cordiano, smiling, was clapping his hands together.

"*Bravo*, Signor Orsini. Nicely done. I see that your father raised you properly. In fact, you are very much like him."

Rafe shot a cold look at the other man. "I assure you, Cordiano, I am nothing like my father."

"It was meant as a compliment, I assure *you*. You are quick. Strong. Fearless. As for your earlier refusal to admit that you wronged my daughter…" The *don* smiled. "That is behind us."

Maybe he'd been mistaken. Maybe coming to Chiara's rescue had been enough to set things straight. Rafe forced an answering smile.

"I'm happy to hear it."

"Gossip can spread as swiftly as a sirocco in a town like this. And people do not forget things that steal one's honor."

Back to square one.

Rafe looked down at the woman who stood in the protective curve of his arm. She was calmer, though he could still feel her trembling. His arm tightened around her. What in hell was he going to do? Of course she was right; as soon as he drove away, the *don* would force her into a marriage, if not with the disgraced Pig Man then with someone else. Some hard-eyed, cold-faced butcher like the ones he'd seen lounging in the castle's entry hall.

Chiara Cordiano would become the wife of a thief and a killer. She would lie beneath him in her marriage bed as he forced her knees apart, grunted and pushed deep inside her….

"All right," Rafe said, the words loud in the stillness of the room.

Cordiano raised an eyebrow. "All right what, Signor Orsini?"

Rafe took a long, seemingly endless breath.

"All right," he said roughly. "I'll marry your daughter."

CHAPTER FIVE

THE private jet Rafe had rented flew swiftly through the dark night.

He'd arranged for the rental at the airport in Palermo. The alternative—a six-hour wait for a commercial flight home—had struck him as impossible.

He had no wish to spend a minute more than necessary on Sicilian soil.

The plane itself was very much like the luxuriously appointed one he and his brothers owned; the pilot and copilot were highly recommended, the cabin attendant pleasant and efficient. She'd made sure he was comfortable, that he had a glass of excellent Bordeaux on the table beside him, that filet mignon would be fine for dinner— not that he was in the mood for dinner—and then she'd faded from sight.

A night flight on a private jet was generally a great place to relax after a difficult day.

But not this time. A muscle in Rafe's cheek ticked.

This time, he was not alone.

A woman was seated across the aisle. Nothing terribly unusual in that. Women had traveled with him before. His PA. His attorney. Clients. His sisters. An occasional mistress, accompanying him for a weekend in Hawaii or Paris.

This woman was none of those things.

She sat wrapped in a black coat even though the cabin was a steady 72 degrees Fahrenheit. She sat very still, her shoulders back, spine rigid. Last he'd looked, her hands were knotted in her lap.

She was an ill-dressed, tight-lipped stranger.

And she happened to be his wife.

Rafe felt the muscle in his cheek jump again.

His wife.

The words, the very concept, were impossible to grasp. He, the man who had no interest in marrying, had married Chiara Cordiano. He'd married a woman he didn't know, didn't like, didn't want, any more than she wanted him.

Rafe shut his eyes, bit back a groan of despair.

How in hell had he let himself get roped into this? Nobody had ever accused him of fancying himself a knight in shining armor. Well, no—but he couldn't have just stood by and let her be handed over to Pig Man.

Assuming, of course, that would really have happened.

Rafe frowned. But would it?

Her father had wanted his daughter to marry an Orsini. The *don* had no way of knowing he was not part of Cesare's organization; Cesare would never have admitted such a thing to an enemy. Cordiano surely would have figured the marriage would strengthen ties between the old world and the new at the same time it settled a debt.

Marrying Chiara to the *capo*, on the other hand, would have accomplished very little, only ensuring a loyalty that already existed. Why waste her on an underling?

Rafe cursed under his breath.

He'd been scammed.

His father had wanted him to marry his old enemy's daughter. Freddo Cordiano had wanted the same thing. But he'd said he wouldn't, and Cordiano had staged a scene straight from a fairy tale. Either the prince married the princess, or the ogre got her.

The only question was, had Chiara known about it?

Rafe folded his arms.

Dutiful Sicilian daughter that she was, what if she'd agreed to do her best to make him think everything that had happened today was real, starting with that ridiculous stuff on the road? A pair of burlesque bandits, stopping his car... Yes. That would have been good staging. Both father and daughter would have known it wouldn't send him running, that if anything, he'd have been even more determined to reach San Giuseppe.

Even that kiss in the car. Her initial struggle against him, followed by that one sweet sigh of surrender, the softening of her lips, the rich, hot taste of her...

He'd been had.

Aside from him, the only other person who hadn't been in on the con was Giglio. Chiara and her old man had used the *capo* as neatly as they'd used him.

Rafe narrowed his eyes.

Final proof? The 1-2-3 wedding ceremony. Cordiano had obviously pulled a bunch of high-powered strings. There'd been no posting of wedding banns, no formalities beyond signing a couple of papers in front of a mayor who'd all but knelt at the *don*'s feet. A handful of mumbled words and, wham, it was done.

Cordiano had beamed. "You may kiss the bride," he'd said.

Except, of course, Rafe hadn't.

Chiara had looked up at him. He'd looked down at her. Her eyes had held no expression; her lips had been turned in. "Do not touch me" had been her message, and he'd come within a heartbeat of saying, "Trust me, baby, you don't have a thing to worry about."

That kiss in the car, that one moment of heat… Easy to explain. The encounter on the road had left him pumping adrenaline. Danger, sex… One complemented the other. A man could fool himself into thinking anything when he was in that kind of state.

Rafe sat up straight.

Okay. He understood it all. Not that it mattered. He'd married the woman. Now he had to unmarry her. Next stop, an annulment. Divorce. Whatever it took.

Problem solved.

Not that he would just abandon his blushing bride. Yes, she'd trapped him, but he wasn't blameless. He, the man who prided himself on logical thinking, had not thought logically. The price for digging yourself out of a hole, even when someone else had handed you the shovel, was never cheap.

He would do the honorable thing. Arrange a financial settlement. Considering all the effort Chiara had gone to, hauling him in, she was entitled to it. Then she could return to Sicily and he could forget all about—

"Signor Orsini."

He looked up. Chiara stood next to him. He tried not to shake his head at the sight. When they were kids, his sister Anna had gone through a Goth period that had, thankfully, lasted only about a minute. She'd dressed in black from head to toe. She'd even dyed her long, blond hair black.

"You look like something the cat dragged in," he'd told her, with all the aplomb of an older brother.

But a cat would not have bothered dragging Chiara in. Or out. She looked too pathetic. Well, except for the hair. Even skinned back in that damned bun again, it had the gloss of a raven's wing.

Was looking like this part of the act?

"Yes?"

Yes?

Chiara forced herself not to show any reaction. Three hours of silence, and the best Raffaele Orsini could come up with was yes, said in a way that almost hung it with icicles?

Still, yes was an improvement. She would try not to show her annoyance.

"*Signor.* We must talk."

His eyes narrowed to dark blue slits. Chiara was puzzled, but then she realized he was considering what she'd said, as if she'd made a request, when what she'd made was a demand.

She wanted to stamp her foot in fury! What an *imbecile*! Did he think she was a stray cat he'd taken in? That she would be so grateful she would simply sit quietly and let him do whatever he wished with her life?

She had not signed herself over to this man.

Yes, she'd married him. Heaven knew she had not wanted to do it, but choosing between going to America with a hoodlum and remaining in San Giuseppe with a killer had made her decision easy.

The only surprise was that he'd gone through with the ceremony, such as it was. She'd spent the last few hours trying to come up with a reason; by now, she had several.

Her father had paid him to do it. *His* father had

paid him to do it. Her father had threatened him with what would happen if he didn't, though she had to admit, that was a slim possibility. Whatever else he was, the American was not a coward.

Perhaps he had finally realized the benefits of marrying the *don*'s daughter. She had no illusions about her feminine appeal: she was mousy, skinny, nothing at all like the voluptuous females who caught men's eyes. What she was, was a link to her father, and thus, to power.

Not that the American's reasons for marrying her mattered.

He'd done it, was what counted, and she'd even felt a rush of gratitude that he had saved her from being given to Giglio—but gratitude only went so far. The bottom line, as they said in all those American movies she watched late at night on TV, was that she had no wish to be married, none to stay married. And from his silence, from the way he looked at her now, she was fairly certain Raffaele Orsini felt the same.

It was time to lay the cards on the table.

She told him exactly that.

"*Signor.* It is time to lay the cards on the table."

One dark eyebrow lifted. He seemed amused. "Whose cards?"

Chiara frowned. "What do you mean, whose cards? *The* cards. Is that not what one lays on the table?"

"Not precisely. They're either your cards or mine." That faint hint of amusement—a smirk, was closer to accurate—disappeared from his face. "Sit down."

"I would rather—"

"Sit," he barked, jerking his chin toward the leather seat angled toward his.

She bristled. Just as she'd suspected. He thought he owned her. Well, he didn't, and the sooner he knew that, the better, but there was no sense in getting sidetracked right now.

"Well?"

He had folded his arms across his chest and sat staring at her, his expression unreadable. He'd discarded his suit coat soon after they'd boarded the plane, stripped away his tie, opened the top two buttons of his white shirt and rolled back his sleeves.

The look on his face, the lack of formality in his clothing, his posture…had he done it deliberately to intimidate her? He looked—he looked very masculine. Aggressive. Those wide shoulders, so clearly defined by the fine cotton of his shirt. The strong, tanned column of his throat. The tanned and muscular forearms…

"Let me know when you're done with the inventory."

Chiara jerked her head up. His tone was silken, that hint of amusement back on his face. She flushed. Why was he making this so difficult? He had not wanted this marriage any more than she. The only reason she had kept silent the last hours was because she'd assumed he would make the first move.

She knew how it was with men like him. They needed to believe they were in charge, even when they weren't.

She drew a breath, then let it out. "What you did—asking me to marry you—"

He snorted. "I didn't ask you anything."

"No. Not if one wishes to be precise, but—"

"I *am* being precise."

"Well, yes. Of course. What I mean is, if you hadn't proposed—"

"You keep getting that wrong, baby. I didn't propose."

"I mean it only as a figure of speech, Signor Orsini."

"And I mean it as fact. I didn't ask. I didn't

propose." His eyes narrowed again. "And yet, surprise, surprise, here we are."

She nodded, but it was not a surprise at all. Never mind all her speculation. He had been sent to marry her and he had done so. All the rest was meaningless.

"So?"

He was waiting. Fine. She just had to phrase this right.

"Here we are indeed," she said politely, as if the topic had to do with finding themselves in the same shop instead of in a plane heading for America. "And…and—"

She hesitated. This was the tricky part. Convincing him he had done all he had to do, that now he could take a step that would free them both, might be a challenge. She had a small fortune to offer him in exchange for a divorce. Her mother had left her all her jewelry. Her mother had never worn any of it. Vanity, she'd said, was a sin. But Mama had not been completely unworldly. She'd hidden her jewels, told Chiara where to find them in case, someday, she should need what they might buy.

Today that time had come.

She had the jewels hidden in the bottom of the

small suitcase she'd packed. The American could have them all if he would grant her her freedom.

Still, she had to phrase her argument properly, not dent his macho ego.

Her throat, her mouth had gone dry. Unconsciously she swept the tip of her tongue lightly over her lips.

"And," she continued, "this isn't what I want. What either of us wants."

He said nothing, and she touched the tip of her tongue to her lips again. Rafe watched her do it, and a fist seemed to close slowly in his belly.

Did she know what she doing? Was the gesture innocent or deliberate? Her tongue was pink. It was a kitten's tongue. It had touched his, however briefly; he could remember the silken feel of it.

She was still talking, but he had no idea what she was saying. His eyes lifted; he studied her face. It was bright with animation. She had, as he'd noticed before, some fairly good features.

Good? The truth was she was beautiful.

Those big violet eyes were fringed by long, thick lashes. The straight little nose was perfectly balanced above a lush, dusty-rose mouth. Her cheekbones weren't just razor sharp, they were carved.

Why did she dress as she did? Why did she hold herself so stiffly? Why did she confine what he now remembered was a silky mane of thick curls in such an unbecoming style? Was it all illusion? Was it part of the scam?

"Why do you wear your hair like that?"

He hadn't meant to ask the question. Obviously, she hadn't expected it. She'd still been talking about something or other. Now she fell silent in midsentence and stared at him as if he'd asked her to explain how to solve a quadratic equation. Then she gave a nervous little laugh.

"I beg your pardon?"

"Your hair. Why do you pull it back?"

To keep her father's men from looking at her the way this man was looking at her now, but she knew better than to tell him that. It wasn't the same thing, anyway. When Giglio and the others looked at her, she felt her skin crawl. But her skin wasn't crawling now. It was…it was…it was tingling.

Chiara's hand flew to her hair. "It's…it's neater this—"

"Let it loose."

The American's voice was rough. His eyes were blue flames. She could see a muscle knotting and unknotting in his cheek.

Suddenly it seemed hard to breathe. "I don't…I don't see any reason to—"

"The reason is that I'm telling you to do it," Rafe said, and a shocked little voice inside him whispered, *What in hell are you doing?*

It was a good question.

He was not a man who believed in ordering women around. He'd explain that, explain that he'd only been joking…

"Let your hair loose, Chiara," he said, and waited.

The seconds crept by. Then, slowly, she put her hands to her hair. The neat bun came undone. Her hair—thick, lustrous, curling—fell down her back.

The fist in his belly tightened again.

"That's better."

She nodded. Cleared her throat. Knotted her hands in her lap.

"As I was saying—"

"It's warm in here."

She swallowed hard. "I don't find it—"

"You don't need that coat."

She looked down at herself, then at him. "I'm…I'm comfortable."

"Don't be silly." He reached toward her, caught the coat's lapels in his hands. "Take it off."

Chiara felt her heart leap. She was alone with

this stranger. Completely alone, in a way she had never been alone with a man before. Enzo, yes. Her father. San Giuseppe's old, half-demented priest. But this was different.

This man was young. He was strong. He was her husband.

That gave him rights. Privileges. She knew about those things, oh God, she knew…

"The coat." His voice was harsh. "Take it off."

Heart pounding, she unbuttoned her coat and shrugged it from her shoulders.

"Listen to me," she said, and hated the way her voice shook. "Signor Orsini. I do not want to be your wife any more than you want to be my husband."

"And?"

"And we are trapped. You had no choice but to marry me and—"

His eyes narrowed again. She had already learned enough about him to know that was not a good sign.

"Is that what you think?"

"Your father wanted it." He said nothing and she hurried on. "And my father wanted it. So—"

"So, I did it to please them both?"

"Yes. No. Perhaps not." She was losing

ground; she could sense it. The thing to do was speak more quickly, make him see that she understood why he'd done what he'd done and that he could gain by undoing it. American gangsters could be bought. She had watched enough films to know a great deal about America, and this was one of the things she knew.

"Perhaps my father made promises to you. Perhaps he said he would reward you."

He sat back. Folded his arms again. Watched her, waited, said nothing, everything about him motionless, his body, his face, nothing moving but that damnable muscle in his cheek.

"Did he offer you a reward, *signor*? I can make a better offer."

The corners of his lips curved. "Can you," he said, very softly.

"As soon as we get to America, we will end the marriage. It is an easy thing to do in your country, yes?"

He shrugged. "And you walk away. From me. From your charming father. From that miserable little town. Everybody lives happily ever after. Right?"

He understood! The relief was enormous. "Yes," she said, with a quick smile. "And you get—"

"Oh, I know what I get, baby. But I'd get that, anyway."

Chiara shook her head. "I don't under—"

"That black thing you're wearing."

Confused, she looked down at herself again, then at him. "The black thing? You mean, my dress?"

"What's under it?"

She blinked. "Under…?"

"Give me a break, okay? You're not deaf. Stop repeating what I say and answer the question. What's under that dress?"

Color heated her face. "My…my undergarments."

He grinned. She almost made the old-fashioned word sound real. "Silk? Lace? Bra? Panties?" His smile tilted. "Or is it a thong?"

Chiara shot to her feet. "You're disgusting!"

"You know, it took me a while but I finally figured it out. This get-up. The clothes, the hair, the 'Don't touch me' all but painted on your forehead—it was all for me, wasn't it?"

She swung away. His hands fell hard on her shoulders and he spun her to him. He wasn't smiling anymore; his face was hard, his eyes cold.

"The real Chiara Cordiano is the one I kissed in that car."

"You are *pazzo*! Crazy! Let go of me. Let go of—"

Rafe bent his head and kissed her. It was a stamp of masculine power and intent, and when she tried to twist away from him, he caught her face between his hands and kissed her even harder, forcing her lips apart, thrusting his tongue into her mouth, taking, demanding, furious with her for the lies, furious with himself for falling for them.

Furious, because he was stupid enough to want to reclaim that one sweet moment when he'd kissed her and she'd responded.

Except, she hadn't.

That, too, had been a lie just like everything else, including the way she was weeping now, big, perfect tears streaming down her face as he drew back.

If he hadn't known better, he'd have bought into the act.

"Come on, baby," he said with vicious cruelty, "what's the point in prolonging this? Get out of that ridiculous dress. Do what you undoubtedly do best." His mouth twisted. "Do it really well and I might just give you that divorce you're after."

"Please," she sobbed, "please..."

"Damn it," Rafe growled. He'd had enough. He reached out with one hand, grabbed the collar of her ugly black dress, tore it open from the neckline to the hem...

And saw white cotton.

Sexless, all but shapeless white cotton. Bra. Panties. The kind of stuff his sisters had worn beneath their school uniforms when they were kids, stuff he and his brothers used to cackle over when they saw those innocent, girlish garments drying on the line in the backyard.

He stood, transfixed, uncertain. Was this, too, part of the act?

"Don't," Chiara whispered, "I beg you, don't, don't, don't..."

Her knees buckled. Rafe cursed, caught his wife in his arms and knew, without question, he'd gotten everything wrong.

CHAPTER SIX

THE cabin spun. The floor tilted. And all Chiara could think was, *No, I am not going to pass out again!*

Once in a lifetime was enough. What she needed to do now was fight, not faint.

The American had scooped her into his arms.

"Stay with me," he was saying. "Come on, baby, stay with me!"

He wanted her conscious when he forced himself on her. That chilling realization was enough to chase the gray fog from her brain. Chiara summoned up all her strength and began beating her fists against his shoulders. One blow connected with his chin, and he captured her flailing hands in one of his and held them tightly against his chest.

"Hey," he said, "take it easy!"

Take it easy? *Take it easy?* Maybe the women in his world gave in, but she would fight to what might well be her last breath because this man was strong. Very strong. No matter what she did, she could not get free.

"Chiara! Listen to me. I'm trying to help you."

"Liar! Liar, liar, li—"

"Damn it, are you crazy?"

No, Rafe thought, answering the question himself. Not crazy. She was blind with panic and he couldn't much blame her. What in hell had he done, all but tearing off her clothes like that? For all she knew, what came next would be—

Hell.

He kept one hand clamped around her wrists, used the other to try and pull the edges of the dress together. It was impossible, especially with her fighting him all the way.

Not exactly the way a man hoped to start his honeymoon. A joke, of course, because this was never going to be a honeymoon but still…

Her head jerked back.

She had some dangerous moves. He had to remember that. The way she could get her knee up, for instance, aiming with precision. Getting in close, putting her off balance, would be his only protection. He swept his arms around her, lifted her off her feet and brought her hard against him.

"Chiara! Stop fighting me!"

The lady was a hellcat personified.

And she was soft. Very soft. Her breasts were flush against his chest. Her belly was against his groin. She was still struggling, moving against him, rubbing against him…

Desperate, Rafe sent a searching glance around him. He needed a place to put her down. Crews on private jets were trained to be discreet but if the attendant chose this minute to see if her passengers wanted something, explaining what was going on might be, at the least, embarrassing.

The Orsini plane had a private bedroom and bathroom in the rear of the cabin. Well, there was a door in the back of this one. He had no idea what was behind it. For all he knew, it might be locked but it was worth—

Chiara's sharp little teeth grazed his throat. Okay. Enough was enough. One bite a day was all she was going to get. Grunting, he upended her, tossed her over his shoulder and strode down the aisle while his crazy wife panted, raged, pounded the hell out of his back. *Please*, he thought grimly when he reached the door, grasped the knob…

Rafe breathed a sigh of relief.

The door opened. And beyond it was some kind of room. Not a bedroom. A lounge. Maybe an office. He rolled his eyes. Who cared what it was? There was a desk. A chair. A small lavatory visible beyond a partly opened sliding door. And, best of all, a small leather sofa just made for accommodating an out-of-control female, he thought, and shouldered the door shut.

He went straight for the sofa. Dumped Chiara on it and stood up.

Bad idea.

She was on her feet and trying to fly past him in a heartbeat. He grabbed her, wrestled her down onto the sofa again, squatted in front of her and clamped his hands around her forearms.

"Listen to me," he said. "I am not going to hurt you."

Chiara bared her teeth. An attack-trained rottweiler might have given him a friendlier response. Rafe shook his head in frustration. He had a mess on his hands and only himself to blame. He'd scared the life out of his bride. A joke to call her that, but that was what she was, at least for the time being.

His fault, sure, but how was he to know she'd

go off like a roomful of high explosives if he touched her?

You didn't just touch her, that sly voice inside him whispered. True. He'd gone at her as if he were out of control, but whose fault was that, if not hers?

A woman couldn't play hot and cold. That kiss this morning. That one moment of incredible surrender. Was he supposed to forget it had happened?

Had it been real? Had it been a ploy to get him on her side? Who in hell knew? And what about the insults she'd heaped on him, her easy assumption that he was a villain, that she could buy him off? Did none of that count for anything?

Yes, but she'd been through a lot today. So had he, but it wasn't the same. He hadn't been threatened with wedded bliss as the wife of her father's *capo*.

If even that had been real. If it hadn't all been an act, meant to make him agree to a marriage a pair of aging *dons* on both sides of the Atlantic seemed to want.

For the moment he'd go with believing his wife hadn't been in on the deal—and why in hell think of her as his wife? She was nothing but a temporary impediment in his life. Maybe she'd calm down once she understood that. Hell, she had to.

He couldn't spend the rest of the flight hanging on to her as she struggled to get away.

Rafe took a long breath.

"Look," he said, "I'm sorry I frightened you. I never— I mean, I had no idea… The thing is, I got angry. And…" And what? None of that excused what he'd done. Truth time, he thought, and drew another breath. "Here's the deal, okay? I thought you had been stringing me along. And—"

"Hah!"

"Hah?"

"Why would I string you along," she panted, "when I would like to string you up?"

How could he want to laugh at a time like this? He couldn't, not without enraging his wildcat even more. Instead he cleared his throat.

"I thought you were part of the plan. You know, to convince me to marry you." Her face registered incredulity, but they were getting somewhere: she had stopped struggling, at least for the moment. "Okay," he said carefully, "I'm going to let go of you. Then I'm going to stand up." His eyes drifted down; he'd all but forgotten her dress was torn in half, showing all that schoolgirl lingerie.

Showing the small but somehow lush breasts, the narrow waist, the flaring hips…

Rafe forced his gaze back to her face. When he spoke, his voice was hoarse.

"I'll stand up, and then I'll get your suitcase so you can change clothes. Okay?"

Chiara glared at him. "I was not part of any plan," she said with icy precision.

"You want something to wear or not?"

He could see her weighing the offer. At last she nodded.

"Good. Fine." Slowly he took his hands from her. She scrambled back as he rose to his feet. She looked like hell, not just the torn dress, but her face was devoid of color, her eyes huge and dark.

And he was the cause.

He, the idiot who'd said yes to marriage to save her, had done this.

"Be right back," he said briskly, striding from the lounge as if shredding a woman's clothes and scaring the life half out of her were just everyday occurrences.

He didn't see her suitcase. Just as well. It was probably overflowing with black dresses and he'd seen enough of them to last a lifetime. He grabbed his carry-on bag, headed back to the lounge…

And paused.

Chiara was exactly where he'd left her, clutching the torn dress together at her breasts. The only difference was in her posture. She sat with her head down, her hair tumbling around her face. The fight had gone out of her; she looked small and vulnerable. Mostly she looked defeated, just as she had in her father's house.

It killed him to see it.

She was shaking. With fear? No, Rafe thought, not this time. He dropped the carry-on bag and hurried to her. She was hovering on the brink of shock. Adrenaline spiked, then dropped, and this was the price you paid.

"Chiara," he said, when he reached her.

She looked up. He could hear her teeth chattering. He cursed softly, went down on his knees and gathered her into his arms.

She balked. He'd expected it and at the first jerk of her muscles, he drew her even closer against him, whispering her name, stroking one big hand gently up and down her back. Gradually he felt her body begin to still.

"That's it," he said softly, his mouth against her temple, his hand still soothing her, and at last she gave a shuddering sigh and leaned into him.

Rafe closed his eyes.

Her face was against his throat. Her lips were

slightly parted. He could feel the delicate whisper of her breath, the warmth of it on his skin.

His arms tightened around her. He drew her from the sofa onto her knees. He felt her hands against his chest, one palm flat against his heart.

She was so small. So delicate. He could feel the fragility of her bones and he thought of the time a migrating songbird had flown into one of the windows that lined the terrace of his penthouse. It had been a windy day; when he heard the soft thud of something hitting the glass, he'd thought it must be a chair cushion, but when he went outside, he found the bird, smaller than seemed possible, lying on the marble floor, eyes glazed, heart beating so frantically that he could see the rise and fall of its feathered breast.

Helpless, clueless, he'd carefully scooped the tiny creature into his palm. Minutes had crept by and just when he was about to give up hope, the bird made a soft peep, scrambled upright, blinked, spread its wings and took to the sky.

Chiara stirred like that now. Her eyes swept over his face.

"Okay?" he said softly.

She swallowed. "Yes."

He felt the same rush of pleasure as the day the

tiny bird had survived its brush with death. Still, he went on holding her in his arms. He didn't want to let her go. She might go into shock again, might need him to comfort her…

"Please let go of me, Signor Orsini."

So much for needing his comfort.

Rafe got to his feet and retrieved the carry-on bag. She was seated on the sofa again, a portrait of composure except for the gaping dress. He cleared his throat, dropped the bag on the floor and jerked his chin at it.

"Nothing in there will really fit you, of course," he said briskly.

"I have my own things. In my suitcase."

"Yeah, well, I grabbed the first bag I saw. Anyway, there's some stuff that might work. Jeans, sweats, a couple of T-shirts…" He was babbling. She could figure things out for herself, once he gave her some privacy. "I'll, ah, I'll wait outside. Let me know when you're done and then…and then, we'll talk. Okay?"

Chiara nodded. Her face gave nothing away, but all things considered, he figured he was doing pretty well. He nodded back, stepped from the room, shut the door, folded his arms…

And waited.

He waited for what seemed a very long time. Just when he'd finally decided she was going to pretend he didn't exist, the door swung open.

His throat constricted.

She was wearing one of his T-shirts over a pair of his workout shorts. The shirt hung to her knees; the shorts fell to midcalf. Her feet were bare. Her hair was a soft cloud of dark chocolate silk: he figured she must have found his brush and used it.

She should have looked comical. At least foolish.

She didn't.

She looked beautiful.

It made him smile. Big mistake. Her chin rose and he knew she was about to give him hell.

"Thank you for the clothes, *signor*."

"It's Rafe."

"Thank you, Signor Orsini," she repeated, and took a deep breath. It made the thin cotton T-shirt fabric lift in a way that drew his gaze to her breasts. "And for this," she said, in a voice that stopped him thinking about the shirt and what was under it. Looking up, he saw the unmistakable glint of steel in her hand. "Touch me again, and I will kill you!"

Well, hell. His brush wasn't the only thing she'd found. She'd found his nail scissors, too.

"Chiara," he said calmly, "put that down."

"Not until we reach New York and you set me free."

"You *are* free." His mouth twisted. "I married you. I didn't buy you."

"I told you. I want an annulment. A divorce. Whatever is legally necessary."

He could feel his temper rising. She was hardly in the position to make demands.

"I have money."

His eyebrows rose. "What?"

"I have my mother's jewels. I told you about them. Obviously, you were not listening." Her eyes met his. "They are very valuable. I will give them to you in exchange for my freedom."

The woman had a wonderful opinion of him. It annoyed him and he told himself to stay calm.

"Do you think this is a bazaar? That you can haggle with me to get what you want?"

Her face colored. "No. I did not mean—" She took a deep breath. "I see what you are trying to do, *signor*. You think, if you direct this conversation elsewhere, you will dissuade me."

He lifted one dark eyebrow. "Dissuade?"

"*Sì.* It means—"

"I know what it means. Someone taught you

some fancy English in that hole-in-the wall town of yours."

"San Giuseppe is not 'my' town," she said coldly. "And yes, Miss Ellis taught me, as you say, some fancy English."

"One of your father's girlfriends?"

She laughed. Miss Ellis had been seventy. Tall, thin, about as approachable as a nun—but the best teacher in the world, until her father had decided she was filling Chiara's head with too much worldly nonsense. It still hurt to remember the day he'd dismissed her.

"One of my tutors," Chiara said, and lifted her chin. "Thanks to her, you will not be able to dissuade me in English or in several other languages."

"Am I supposed to be impressed?"

"You are supposed to be warned, Signor Orsini. I am not prepared to take what has been forced upon me by you and my father standing up."

Rafe grinned. He couldn't help it. For all he knew, she spoke a dozen languages but there was a difference between speaking English like a native and speaking it like a scholar, especially when the words came from the mouth of a woman who looked like an armed street urchin.

"You find this amusing, *signor*? I promise, I will defend myself if you approach me again."

He thought about going straight at her and snatching the scissors away. He wouldn't get hurt—it would be like taking candy from a baby—but what the hell, this was just getting interesting.

"So, you want out of our marriage."

"It is not a marriage, it is an alliance between my father and yours."

"Whatever," he said, as if he didn't know damned well she was probably right. He made a show of shaking his head. "I guess modern women just don't believe in keeping their vows anymore."

Chiara clucked her tongue. "Such nonsense! Neither of us wants this marriage and you know it."

For some reason her certainty irked him. "And you know this about me because…?"

Her eyes narrowed. The tip of her tongue came out and touched her top lip, then swept back inside, to be replaced by a delicate show of small—and, he knew—sharp white teeth that sank, with great delicacy, into her bottom lip.

His gut knotted. His entire body tensed. Ridiculous, but then, the entire day had been ridiculous. Why should things become normal now?

"I mean," he said, sounding like the voice of

reason, "I'm Italian. What if I don't believe in divorce?"

What if the sun went nova? He wasn't Italian, except by heritage. He was American. That was how he thought of himself. And while he didn't believe people should bounce in and out of matrimony, he did believe in divorce when no other solution made sense.

Like now, when they'd both been forced into a union neither wanted…which was exactly what she'd said.

Yes, but why make this easy for her?

He'd been suckered into this. Even if she hadn't been party to the plan, she hadn't protested it, either. Now she wanted out. Fine. So did he. But first he wanted some answers. And this woman—his wife—was the only one who could provide them.

"I'm waiting, baby. Why should I agree to a divorce? After all, I flew across the ocean to marry you."

Chiara blinked. "But you told my father—"

"I know what I told him. I said I had no wish to marry you." Rafe shrugged. "Any good businessman knows better than to accept the first offer when he's negotiating a deal."

"A deal?" She stared at him in disbelief. "You mean—you mean, you intended to go through with it all the time? You only let my father think he could hand me off to that...that animal?"

"I didn't say that."

"You implied it."

First, *dissuade*. Now, *implied*. Tricky words, even for native English speakers, which Chiara was not. What she was, his scissors-wielding bride, was a font of surprises.

"I married you," he said calmly. "Never mind my reasons. As for you...I didn't see Daddy holding a shotgun on you during the ceremony."

"I do not understand what that means."

"It means you married me without a word of argument."

"I would have married a...a donkey if it meant I didn't have to marry Giglio!"

"You're no prize package either, baby."

Color rushed into her cheeks. "You know what I mean. And do not call me 'baby.' I am a grown woman."

Yes. She was. A beautiful grown woman, but there was much more to her than that.

Her face wasn't just lovely, it was animated. Her eyes weren't just a color that reminded him of violets, they were bright with intelligence. He'd seen enough of her body to know it was feminine and lush, but it was the proud way she held herself that impressed him, something in her stance that said she would fight to the end for what she believed.

She was, as she said, a grown woman.

His woman.

His wife.

Rafe felt his body stir. They were alone, still a few hours from landing. He'd scared the hell out of her by coming at her with all the subtlety of a hormone-crazed bull, but then, he'd misjudged her.

She wasn't a femme fatale; she was inexperienced. After all, how many lovers could a woman have in a town the size of San Giuseppe? Cesare had described her as a virgin, but obviously that was impossible. There were no virgins in today's world, not even tucked away in remote towns in the Sicilian hills.

No, things had not gone well a little while ago, but whether his wife wanted to admit it or not, she had responded to him when he'd kissed her before. She'd let him hold her in his arms. All he had to do was take those stupid scissors from her, gather her close, kiss her, slip his hand under that T-shirt…

Was he insane? For one thing, this woman was *not* his wife. Well, she was, but not for long. For another, sleeping with her would only complicate things.

Besides, if he touched her, she'd come apart in terror.

Her reaction to him hadn't been an act. It hadn't been because he hadn't used any finesse. She'd been out of her mind with fear. Real, honest fear. Something awful had happened to her. Something had hurt her so much that she hid inside those godawful black dresses.

Who had done this to her? A man, surely. Giglio? One of the other brutes her father employed?

Hot rage swept through him. He told himself he'd feel this about the violation of any woman, that it had nothing to do with Chiara in particular.

The hell it didn't.

She was his. Temporarily, until he could figure out what to do with her, her but for now she belonged to him. And he was a man who would always protect what was his.

"Chiara."

She looked at him.

"Who hurt you?"

She stared at him. The color drained from her face. "I do not know what you mean."

"Yeah, you do. Why did you scream when I touched you?"

"What you mean is, why didn't I melt with delight."

The words dripped venom, but she wasn't going to put him off that easily. Rafe folded his arms over his chest. "It's a simple question. What made you so frightened of men?"

"What you mean is, why am I unwilling to let men have their way with me?"

"How about not telling me what I mean and just answering the question? What are you afraid of?"

"If we play a round of Twenty Questions, do I win a divorce?"

He was in front of her in two strides. Her hand shot up, the little scissors glinting. Rafe didn't bother playing games. He caught her wrist, took the scissors from her and tossed them on the sofa.

"One question," he said brusquely, "and I want an answer. Why are you afraid of sex?"

"I am not afraid. Besides, what I am or am not is none of your business."

The woman was impossible! "It's every bit my business," he said sharply. "You're my wife."

She laughed. Hell, he couldn't blame her. Sure, a small-town official owned by her father had mumbled some words at them, but the truth was, she was no more his wife than he was her husband.

Except, he was. He had a piece of gilt-edged paper tucked inside his passport case that proved it.

"Was it because you thought I was going to—" he felt his face heat "—to force you?" He cupped her elbows. "Because I wasn't. I got rough, yeah, and I shouldn't have, but I would never have taken you against your will." Her eyes called him a liar; he couldn't much blame her for that, either. "It's the truth. I'm no saint, but I'd never force a woman to make love with me."

"Love," she said, with a little snort of disdain.

"That's what men and women do. They make love." His hands tightened on her. "I'd never sleep with a woman who didn't want me."

No, Chiara thought, no, he wouldn't have to.

A woman would go to him willingly. Raffaele Orsini was all the things women supposedly wanted in a man. He was strong, good-looking and so masculine there were moments he made her feel dizzy.

So, if a woman liked sex, she would like him.

And there were women who liked sex. She was not a fool. She understood that, even though she would never want to be one of those women.

No matter what he claimed, sex was for the man. A woman had to go along with it, if she married. The nudity. The intimacy. The slap of flesh against flesh, the smell of sweat, the terrible, painful, humiliating invasion of your body…

Her mother had explained it all so that she would be prepared if—when—it came time for her to take a husband. "I would not wish my daughter to go to her wedding night without knowing what awaits her," Mama had said.

A shudder went through her. The American saw it. Big, brave, macho creature that he was, he reacted instantly.

"Chiara."

She shook her head, stepped back, but he put his arms around her and drew her against him. She let him do it; the sooner she convinced him she was fine, the sooner he'd let her go.

She could feel the heat coming from him. Feel the hardness of his male body. Smell his male scent. Fear clogged her throat. He seemed to know it and he began whispering to her as he had a few minutes ago. She had to admit he had calmed her then, but she'd been in a state of shock. It was his warmth that had steadied her.

She told herself that a blanket would have had the same effect.

Still, she felt herself responding to his soothing touch, to his voice. She sighed, shut her eyes, felt one of his hands thread into her hair, cup her head, lift her face to his…

Chiara jerked back. "Do not touch me!"

Rafe lifted his hands from her with exaggerated care. She was looking at him as if he was a serial killer. Undoubtedly, the lady had a problem. But it wasn't his problem. *She* wasn't his problem. The minute they reached New York, he'd phone his lawyer and tell her to get started on whatever had to be done to end this sham of a marriage.

The sooner he was out of this mess, the better.

CHAPTER SEVEN

CHIARA'S first glimpse of New York City almost took her breath away.

Lights, what seemed like millions of them, lay winking beneath the plane like sparkling diamonds on black velvet. As the jet dropped lower, she could see that the lights were moving. They were lights from automobiles racing along endless intersecting highways.

Where were all these people going in the middle of the night? It *was* the middle of the night, American time. East Coast time. She would have to remember that. This was not like Italy, where the hour was the same if you were in Rome or Florence or Palermo.

Not that she'd ever been to Rome or Florence. Not that she'd ever been anywhere.

It should have been exciting, the realization that she was about to land on another continent, in a city she'd read of and dreamed about. But it wasn't.

It was terrifying.

She wasn't here by choice, she was here as the unwilling bride of a stranger. She knew nothing about her husband. No, she thought, swallowing hard as the plane descended, that was not true. She did know something about him. She knew that he was a man who bore her father's stamp of approval.

That could only mean he was a hoodlum, just like her father.

Except—except, he wasn't really like her father. He could be cold and hard, but sometimes there was a tenderness to him, too. And he was beautiful. She knew it was a strange word to use to describe a man but none other suited him. His height. His body. His face, *Dio*, his face, those hard, masculine angles and planes, that firm mouth…

Firm. Warm. And soft, so soft against hers…

The plane touched down, bumping delicately against the runway. The captain made a pleasant announcement, welcoming them to New York. Chiara, fumbling with her seat belt, rose quickly to her feet. The plane was still moving along the taxiway as she started blindly up the aisle.

A strong hand closed lightly on her elbow.

"I'm happy to see you're in such a hurry to reach your new home," her husband said.

She could hear the derision in his voice, feel the possessiveness of his grasp. Her heart thumped.

God only knew what lay ahead.

Whatever it was, she would face it with courage. If life had taught her anything, it was that you must never show weakness to your oppressor.

Finally the plane came to a stop. The door shushed open. Chiara stepped out into the North American night.

She'd heard all about security procedures, but they evidently didn't apply to powerful American gangsters. Her husband led her into a small building. He presented their passports to a man who hardly glanced at them. Minutes later they made their way out to a waiting automobile. A uniformed driver stood beside it.

Her steps faltered and her husband's hand tightened on her elbow.

"Keep moving," he said coldly.

As if she had a choice.

What had the poet said in the *Divine Comedy*? Something about abandoning hope, all those who entered here.

One last, free breath and Chiara stepped into the back of the limousine.

The big car moved swiftly through the night.

So far, so good, Rafe thought—assuming you discounted the fact that his wife was sitting beside him like a prisoner being driven to her execution.

At least there hadn't been a reception committee waiting, something he'd half expected. He'd figured Cordiano would have phoned his father. Cesare would have told the family....

What fun that would have been.

The old man gloating. His mother going from being upset that there hadn't been a big wedding to planning a party that would rival anything Manhattan had ever seen. His sisters teasing him unmercifully. And his brothers...

Lord, his brothers! Better not even to go there.

But the reception committee hadn't materialized. Clearly, Cordiano had not contacted Cesare. Rafe had no idea why, and frankly he didn't much care. What mattered was that he had some breathing room. Tomorrow morning, first thing, he'd call his lawyer, start the procedure that would return his life to normal. No matter what he'd told Chiara, he wanted a divorce every bit as much as she did.

The drama on the plane, all that stuff about not giving her a divorce? Meaningless. He'd been ticked off, that was all, and he'd made a threat he had no intention of keeping.

He wanted out.

Traffic was light, this time of night. The big car moved smoothly along the highway, sped along Fifth Avenue and drew to a stop before his building. The doorman greeted them politely; if he found the sight of a woman wrapped in a coat like the kind old ladies wore in bad foreign films unusual, he was too well trained to let it show.

"Do you need help with your bags, Mr. Orsini?"

I need help with my life, Rafe thought, but he tossed him a polite "No, thanks" and headed for his private elevator, his carry-on hanging from his shoulder, Chiara's old-fashioned leather suitcase clutched in one hand, the other wrapped around her elbow. It would have made things easier to let go, but he knew better.

The last thing he needed tonight was to end up running down Fifth Avenue after her.

They rode the elevator in silence. Nothing new there. They'd made the trip from the airport the same way. The door slid open when they reached his penthouse. Rafe stepped from the car. Chiara didn't. He rolled his eyes and quick-stepped her into the foyer. The elevator door shut; Rafe sent it to the lobby level and let go of his wife's arm.

"Okay," he said briskly, "we're home."

He winced. What a stupid remark, but what else was there to say? He dropped their bags, shrugged off his jacket, checked the little stack of mail on the table near the entryway, checked his voice mail, gave Chiara time to say something, do something, but when he turned around she was standing precisely where he'd left her, except she'd backed up so that her shoulders were pressed against the silk-covered wall.

She looked exhausted and terrified, lost in the awful black coat. Defiance, or an attempt at it, glittered in her wide eyes, but the overall effect was—there was no other word for it—pathetic.

Despite himself, he felt a surge of pity along with the gnawing realization that there was no point in being angry with her. Never mind his accusations. The truth was unavoidable. Neither of them had wanted this marriage.

She was as trapped as he. More so, maybe. He, at least, was on his own turf. She, however, was in a place she didn't know, a country she didn't know…

Hell, he thought, and cleared his throat. "Chiara?" She looked at him. "Why don't you, ah, why don't you take off your coat?"

She didn't answer. Okay. He'd try again.

"Would you, ah, would you like something to eat?"

Nothing. His jaw tightened. She wasn't going to help him one bit.

"Look," he said, "I know this isn't what either of us wanted—"

"It is what *you* wanted," she said coldly.

"Me? Hell, no. Why would you think—"

"You won't agree to a divorce."

"Yeah. Right." Rafe ran his hand through his hair. "Look, about that—"

"The one thing I promise you, *signor*, is that I will never be a real wife to you!"

"Damn it, if you'd just listen—"

"You can force me to remain your property." Her chin rose. "You can force me to do a lot of things, but I will never let you forget that I do them unwillingly."

Rafe's eyes narrowed. "Are we back to talking about sex?"

The rush of color to her cheeks was answer enough. Why did her vow make him so angry?

He had no intention of taking her to bed. Why would he when he could scroll through his BlackBerry and find the names of a dozen women who'd sleep with him and be happy about it? Beautiful women. Sexy women. Women who'd make this one look like Little Orphan Annie.

"I am talking about female compliance in general and, yes, that would include—it would include—"

"Sex." He smiled tightly. "You can say the word. It won't pollute you."

Her color went from deep pink to bright red. "I know it is difficult for you to believe, but not every woman wants to pretend she enjoys being the recipient of a man's most base desires."

Whoa. Her attitude definitely needed updating, but that would be some other man's problem, not his. Why not tell her she had nothing to worry about? Divorce was just a phone call away—

"Perhaps you think you are entitled to…to special privileges because you supposedly saved me from Giglio."

Whatever hackles were, he could damn near feel his rise. "Supposedly?"

Chiara shrugged. "You said it yourself. You had every intention of marrying me all along."

"I said that because I was angry. You know damned well I only did it because your old man threatened to hand you over to his *capo*."

"Why should I believe you now?" Her smile was like ice. "After all, *signor*, you lie with such ease."

Okay. Enough. He'd taken one insult too many. It was time to let the lady stew in her own juices for a while.

"You know," he said coldly, "I've had enough of this nonsense to last a lifetime. It's bedtime."

All the color drained from her face. She'd misunderstood him. He opened his mouth to explain, but before he could say a word, she spat out a Sicilian phrase he'd never heard anywhere but on the streets of his youth.

"Right," he said through his teeth, "that's precisely what I am."

He strode purposefully toward her, grabbed her arm and yanked her toward him. She cried out, struggled, and on a curse the equal of hers, he lifted her into his arms and carried her up the staircase to the second floor, down the hall and into one of the guest rooms where he dumped her in the center of the bed.

She scrambled back against the pillows. Her hair was a tangle of wild curls. Her ugly coat had come open, exposing her ludicrous outfit…

Her amazingly sexy outfit.

Her breasts, shadowed beneath the thin cotton of his T-shirt. Her nipples, pebbled and just waiting for the touch of his fingers, the heat of his mouth…

Rafe stepped back. Jerked his head toward a half-open door.

"Your bathroom's through there. There's a clean toothbrush in the vanity. Toothpaste. Towels. Soap. Shampoo. Whatever else you might need."

"If you think I'm going to…to prepare myself for you—"

"If you did, you'd be wasting your time. I like my women soft, feminine and sexy. You don't even approach that description. No wonder your old man had to find you a husband."

It was a good line, and he made the most of it by walking out.

He was halfway down the hall when he heard her door slam hard enough to rattle the walls. For some crazy reason, it made him smile.

A hot shower, then bed.

That was what he needed.

The shower was fine. So was the bed until he turned the sheets into a tangled mess. After an hour of trying to sleep, he gave up, lay back and watched the digital alarm clock blink away the minutes.

Two a.m. Three. Four. Damn it, he had to be at work in the morning. He didn't have time for this.

Maybe he ought to phone his lawyer now. Yeah, it was the middle of the night, but so what? He had Marilyn Sayers on retainer. A big, fat retainer. The whole point of it was so that he could contact her anytime, anyplace, about anything....

Rafe got out of bed, pulled on a pair of old gray sweatpants. What difference would it make if he spoke to Sayers now or later? She was a top-notch legal eagle; this was a simple divorce. An hour or two wouldn't mean a thing.

He'd wait.

He thought about going for a run in the park, but that would have meant leaving Chiara alone in the apartment. Somehow, that didn't seem wise. He had a bottle of sleeping tablets in the medicine cabinet, something the doctor had given him a couple of years ago after minor surgery on his knee—he'd torn a tendon in a motorcycle accident. But he'd never taken even one of the pills and he wasn't about to start now.

A shot of brandy. That would do it.

It did.

Twenty minutes after he drank the Courvoisier, Rafe got into bed and tumbled into sleep.

Something woke him.

He wasn't sure what it was. A sound, but what? Not his alarm. The red numbers on the clock were steady at 5:05 a.m., which meant he had fifty-five minutes until the thing went off.

There it was again. A noise. Faint but... A cry? That was it. A cry. Weeping.

Hell. It was Chiara.

He sat up in bed, rubbed his hands over his stubbled jaw and cheeks. Now what? Did he ignore it? Might as well. Let her cry. Who gave a damn? Every time he tried to treat her with kindness, she reacted like a junkyard dog.

He lay back against the pillows again, stacked his arms beneath his head. She was unhappy? He wasn't exactly ecstatic. If she was crying, it was her business.

But it didn't stop. Well, so what? He'd heard women cry before. Ingrid, for example, just a couple of days ago… Just a lifetime ago. But it hadn't been like this. Sad. Desperate. As if the sobs were being torn from Chiara's soul.

Rafe threw back the covers, got to his feet, headed for the door and then for the guest suite, where he paused. "Chiara?"

At first he thought the sobs had stopped. They hadn't. They'd just grown muffled. She was crying as if her heart might break.

"Chiara," he said again, and tapped lightly on the door. Still no answer. He took a breath. Then, carefully, he tried the knob.

It turned, and the door swung open.

The room was in darkness, but she'd left the bathroom light on and the door partly open. He could see the huddled form visible in the center of the bed.

Rafe called her name again. Still, no answer. Slowly, certain he was going to regret this, certain she'd rear up, scream the bloody building down when she realized he was in her bedroom, he made his way forward and sat down, gingerly, on the edge of the mattress. He could see her now, part of her, at least; she was just a small, sad lump under the duvet, on her belly, her face buried against the pillows.

His heart constricted. She was small and frightened and he'd known that and added to it.

Without thinking, he reached out and laid his hand gently against her hair.

"Chiara, sweetheart, I'm sorry. Please, don't cry…"

The bedclothes seemed to explode. Rafe braced himself for a scream, a shout, a right to the jaw… But none of that happened. Chiara launched herself at him, wound her arms around his neck and buried her damp face against his naked shoulder.

Stunned, he sat absolutely still. Then, slowly, he slipped his arms around her. Filled them with soft, warm, trembling woman.

He shut his eyes.

Holding her felt wonderful. And she smelled good. His soap. His shampoo. And mingling with their scents, essence of woman. Of Chiara.

Of his wife.

His body stirred. Silently he cursed himself for it. There was nothing sexual happening here. Dawn was about to break over a sleeping city and he had a weeping woman in his arms.

Remember that, Orsini, he told himself sternly.

"Chiara," he said gently. "What is it? Did you have a nightmare?"

She nodded. Her hair, all those dark and lovely curls, slid like feather wisps against his skin. He shut his eyes again, drew her closer, held her more tightly against his heart.

"Do you want to talk about it?"

She shook her head.

"No. Okay. Fine. You don't have to—"

"I dreamed it was my wedding night."

A muscle knotted in his jaw. It *was* her wedding night. A hell of a thing to know that *he* was her nightmare.

"It's all right, baby. Nothing will happen to you. I promise."

"My wedding night with…with Giglio."

A nightmare, all right. Rafe's arms tightened around her.

"Shh, sweetheart. It was just a bad dream."

A shudder went through her. "It was so real. His hands on me. His mouth."

"Shh," Rafe said again, an unreasoning rage filling him at the picture she'd painted. "Giglio can't get to you. Not anymore."

Silence. Another shudder. Then, a whisper so low he could hardly hear it.

"What?" he said, and bent his head closer to hers.

"I said…I said I have been awful to you,

Raffaele. You saved me from him. And instead of saying thank you, I have accused you of…of all kinds of terrible things."

He smiled. "Seems to me we've done a pretty good job of accusing each other of all kinds of terrible things."

"It is only that I never expected any of this to happen. My father had threatened to marry me to an American but—"

"Just what every guy hopes," Rafe said, trying to lighten things. "To be a beautiful woman's worst nightmare."

His little attempt at humor flew straight over her head. "No," she said quickly, "I did not dream of you, Raffaele, I dreamed of—"

"I know. I only meant… Chiara, you have to believe me. My father wanted me to marry you, yes, but I didn't have any intention of doing it. Not that a man wouldn't be lucky to marry you," he added quickly, "but—"

Her hand lifted; she placed her fingers lightly over his lips.

"It…it isn't that I don't want to be your wife. It's that I do not want to be any man's wife. Do you understand?"

He didn't. Not really. He'd been dating women

since he'd turned sixteen and he'd never yet come across one whose ultimate goal, no matter what she claimed, wasn't marriage.

Then he thought of what he knew of the woman in his arms. Her father's domination. Her isolation. Above everything else, her fear of sex, a fear he'd done little to ease over the past several hours.

"Truly," she said, "it is not you. It would be any man." She drew back in his arms, her face turned up to his, her eyes brilliant, her dark lashes spiky with tears. "Do you see?"

God, she was so beautiful! So vulnerable, lying back in his arms…

"Yes," he said, his voice a little rough, "I do see. But you need to know—you need to know not all men are beasts, sweetheart."

A wan smile curved her lips. "Perhaps you are the exception."

The exception? If he were, his body wouldn't be responding to the tender warmth of hers. He wouldn't be looking at her and wondering if her mouth tasted as sweet as he remembered, if she was naked under the oversize cotton thing he assumed was a nightgown.

"I…I appreciate your decency," she said, and

every miserable male instinct he owned shrieked, *Yeah? Then how about proving it?*

He sat up straight, all but tore Chiara's encircling arms from his neck and set her back against the pillows, grateful—hell, hopeful—that his baggy sweats would hide the effect she'd had on him.

"Well," he said brightly, "you'll be okay now." She didn't answer. "So, ah, so try to get some sleep." Still no answer. He cleared his throat. "Chiara? About that divorce?"

"Yes?"

The hopeful note in the single word would have thrilled him if this were Ingrid or any one of a hundred other women. As it was, it only made him feel a pang of remorse.

"I'll phone my attorney first thing in the morning and get it started."

She gave a deep sigh. "*Grazie bene*, Raffaele. The jewels—"

"Forget about them. They're yours."

"I can, at least, use them to pay my share of the legalities."

"I said, I don't want them." He knew he sounded harsh but, damn it, did she really think he'd let her pay for the severance of their marriage? Okay, it was a bogus marriage but still… "I'd prefer you keep them," he said, trying for a calmer tone.

"*Grazie.* I can use the money they bring to live on. New York is expensive, yes?"

"New York is expensive, yes. But it won't be so bad. Not with alimony."

"Alimony?"

Alimony? his baffled brain echoed. A settlement was bad enough but alimony? Why would he pay alimony to a woman who'd been his wife for, what, twenty-four hours?

"I do not expect alimony, Raffaele. We have not had a real marriage."

"Yeah, but this is America. Everybody pays alimony," he said with a straight face, even though he could already hear his lawyer screaming in legal horror.

Chiara smiled. "I think," she said, very softly, "I think, perhaps, you are an honorable man, Raffaele Orsini."

Guilt made his jaw tighten. She wouldn't think that if she could see the response of his body to the soft hand she laid upon his thigh. He took that hand, gave it a brisk little shake and stood up.

"Okay," he said brightly, "sleep time."

Her smile faded.

"You won't have that bad dream again," Rafe said softly. She didn't answer and he cleared his throat. "If you like—if you like, I'll sit in that chair until you doze off."

"Would you mind?"

"Mind? No. I'm happy to do it."

"It would be comfortable for you?"

Comfortable? Not in this lifetime. The chair in question was a Queen Anne, a Marie Antoinette, a Lady Godiva or something like that. It was puny looking. He'd put his own stamp on the living room, the library, the dining room and his bedroom, but he'd grown impatient after a while and turned the interior decorator loose on the guest rooms. One result was this chair. It might hold a dwarf but would it hold a man who stood six-three in his bare feet?

"Raffaele? I would not want you to be uncomfortable."

"I'll be fine," he said with conviction, and he pulled the chair forward, sank onto it and prayed it wouldn't collapse under his weight.

"*Grazie bene,*" Chiara said softly.

Rafe nodded. "No problem," he said briskly. "You just close your eyes and—"

She was asleep.

He sat watching her for a while, the dark curve of her lashes against her pale cheeks, the tumble of her curls against her face, the steady rise and fall of her breasts. A muscle knotted in his jaw, and he reached out and tugged the duvet up, settled it around her shoulders.

He wanted to touch her. Her face. Her hair. Her breasts.

Determinedly he forced his brain from where it was heading. Concentrated on taking deep breaths. He needed to get some rest but it was impossible. The damned chair…

What if he slipped out of the room? She was deep, deep asleep. Yes, but what if she dreamed of Giglio again? He'd promised she wouldn't, but thus far, his clever predictions had hardly been infallible.

His back ached. His butt. His legs. He looked at the bed. It was king-size. Chiara was curled on one edge. He could sit at a distance from her—sit, not lie—and at least stretch his legs. He wouldn't touch her and she'd never know he was there.

Rafe made the switch carefully, waiting to make sure she didn't awaken before he leaned back against the pillows. Yes. That was much better. He knew he wouldn't sleep even though he was exhausted. He yawned. Yawned again until his jaws creaked. Maybe he'd just shut his eyes for a couple of minutes....

The sun, streaming in through the terrace doors, jolted him awake.

Chiara lay fast asleep in his arms, her hand over his heart, her breath soft and warm against his throat.

Rafe's body clenched like a fist. He knew the perfect way to wake her. He'd kiss her hair, her eyelids, her mouth. Slowly her lashes would lift. Her beautiful eyes would meet his.

"Chiara," he'd whisper, and instead of jerking back, she'd say his name, lift her hand to his face, and he'd turn his head, press his mouth to her palm, then to the pulse beating in the hollow of her throat, then to her breasts, breasts that he was now damned sure had never known a man's caress—

Rafe swallowed a groan of frustration. Then he dropped the lightest of kisses on his sleeping wife's hair, left her bed and headed to his bathroom for the longest cold shower of his life.

CHAPTER EIGHT

SLOWLY, cautiously, Chiara opened her eyes.

Had she been dreaming, or had Raffaele been in bed with her, holding her in his arms?

It must have been a dream. A man wouldn't get into a woman's bed only to hold her close. Not even a man like Raffaele, who—she had to admit—seemed to have some decent instincts. Even he would not have slept with her curled against him without…without trying to do something sexual.

And yet the dream had seemed real.

His arms, comforting and strong around her. His body, warm and solid against hers. His heart, beating beneath her palm. And then, just before she awakened, the soft brush of his lips…

A dream, of course. And, at least, not a dream that had sent her into a panic.

Despite the things about him that were good—his gallantry in marrying her, his gentleness last night—he still represented everything she despised.

But she no longer despised him.

What if he'd actually slept with her in his arms? If she'd awakened, wrapped in his heat? If she had looked up at him, clasped the back of his head, brought his lips to hers…

Chiara shoved aside the bedcovers and rose quickly to her feet. There was a cashmere afghan at the foot of the bed. She wrapped herself in it and padded, barefoot, over a rich Oriental carpet to the doors that opened onto a small terrace.

The morning air was crisp, the colors of the trees across the street, brilliant. Was that Central Park? It had to be. It surprised her. She knew of the park, of course, but she had not expected such an oasis of tranquillity.

Pedestrians hurried along the sidewalk: kids dressed for school, men and women in business suits, sleepy-looking people in jeans and sweats being tugged along by dogs hurrying to reach the next lamppost. Cars, taxis and buses crowded the road.

The street was busy. Still, it was surprisingly quiet up here.

She hadn't expected that, either.

The truth was, she hadn't expected most of what had happened since yesterday. She certainly hadn't expected what little she'd discovered about Raffaele Orsini.

She had, almost certainly, misjudged his reasons for marrying her. She felt a little guilty about that. Not a lot. After all, they had misjudged each other. But everything pointed to the fact that he had not gone to Sicily to do his father's bidding.

That he had taken her as his wife only to save her from being given to Giglio.

But, as he had said, he was no Sir Galahad. He was a hoodlum, like her father. Like his father. It was in his blood, even though he looked more like a man who'd stepped out of one of the glossy magazines that had been Miss Ellis's one weakness....

Or like the *David*. Michelangelo's marble masterpiece. She had never actually seen the statue, of course, but one of her tutors had taught her about art, had shown her a photo of the *David* in a book...

Chiara swallowed dryly.

Did Raffaele look like that statue? Was his naked body that perfect? Was all of him so...so flagrantly, blatantly, beautifully male?

Beautifully male?

Blindly she turned and hurried back into the bedroom.

What did it matter? He could look like one of God's angels and it wouldn't change the fact that he was what he was. That he did things, made his money—lots of money, from what she'd seen of his life so far—doing things she didn't want to think about.

That he had decent instincts was interesting, even surprising, but it didn't change the facts.

Still, would it not be a good thing to make it clear she was grateful to him for what he had done? She remembered little of what they'd said to each other when he'd come into her room last night. She was pretty sure she'd said thank you, but showing her gratitude would be polite.

How?

She could find ways to make herself useful.

Yes. Of course. She could be useful. He had no wife. Well, he had her but she was not really his wife. The point was, there was no woman here to do things. Clean. Cook. She could do those things. She could start immediately. She could make breakfast. Make coffee.

Coffee! Men liked awakening to the scent of

it. When her father came down in the morning, he always said the smell of good, fresh espresso was the perfect way to start a day.

Chiara tore a dress and underwear from her suitcase, rushed into the bathroom and turned on the shower.

Rafe always began the day with a shower.

He began this one with two, both icy enough to make his teeth chatter.

The frigid water did the job of quieting his still-jumpy hormones, but nothing could stanch the headache that had settled in just behind his eyes.

He downed two ibuprofen but the trolls inside his skull only laughed and drummed harder.

The headache matched his rapidly deteriorating mood. Was he crazy? He had to be, otherwise why was he taking this Boy Scout routine so far? Bad enough he'd married Chiara. What in hell had possessed him to sleep with her? To really *sleep* with her—no euphemism involved.

Waking up in bed with a woman you couldn't have plastered against you and a hard-on you didn't want in your sweats was not a good idea, especially if you were stuck with the woman and unable to do anything about the hard-on.

Uh-uh. Definitely not a way to begin the day.

And when, exactly, had he turned so accepting of the mess he was in?

Rafe glared as he stepped out of the shower stall and toweled off.

Not just a Boy Scout. At the rate he was going, he was pushing for the Order of the Arrow with oak leaf clusters. And for what reason? He'd done his good deed for her. Now, he'd do a good deed for himself.

Divorce court, next stop.

Absolutely, it was time to phone his lawyer. First, though, he needed to get his head working right. A couple of aspirin, to help move the ibuprofen along. Then coffee. Lots of coffee. Strong and black. That would do it.

When a man put, what, eight, nine thousand miles on his internal clock in twenty-four hours and got married to a woman he didn't want, that man definitely needed something to bring him down. Mileage and a marriage. It sounded like one of those self-help books, but what it was, was the reason he wasn't thinking straight.

Why else would he have suddenly felt such compassion, okay, such tenderness for the babe who'd screwed up his life?

Wanting to make it with her? That was under-standable. He was male. She was female and under those crazy outfits she wore, she wasn't bad-looking. Yeah, but there was no way in the world he'd follow through on those most basic of male instincts.

He didn't know much about matrimonial law but what little he did know told him that, as of now, their quickie set of I do's could be erased in a heartbeat. No sex? No real marriage.

Sleep with the lady and that would change.

Besides, why would he want to sleep with her? She was afraid of sex. What man wanted a scared woman in his bed? Plus, she was a virgin. No question about it anymore.

Imagine. In this day and age, she was a virgin.

Rafe grimaced as he stepped into a pair of faded jeans.

He'd been with a lot of women but never with a virgin. Any man with half a functioning brain knew to avoid that situation, because taking a woman's virginity was a trap. It left you with the kind of responsibility he most assuredly did not need and did not want.

He zipped his fly, pulled on a gray cotton sweater. He didn't bother shaving. No point pretending he'd go to his office today. Nothing on his desk was as important as dissolving a relationship that wasn't a relationship.

He checked the time. It was barely seven. A reasonable hour at which to phone Marilyn Sayers, but first he'd have that coffee. Let the headache tablets do their thing. He wanted to sound cool and controlled when he told Sayers about his incredible situation. She would have questions, but all she really needed to know was where and when the marriage had taken place and that he wanted out, ASAP.

Marriage? He snorted. Ridiculous. He wouldn't dignify what had happened in San Giuseppe by calling it that. There'd been some kind of ceremony, that was all.

It sure as hell hadn't been a—

Crash!

Rafe spun toward the door. What was that? It sounded as if a two-car collision had just taken place in his apart—

There it was again, a metallic crash loud enough to make the trolls inside his skull pick up the tempo. By the time the third crash echoed through the penthouse, he was halfway down the stairs, racing down the hall...

He skidded to a stop in the entrance to his kitchen. What the hell…?

It looked as if Bloomingdale's housewares department had decided to hold a sale right here, in his pristine—his once pristine—kitchen. The white granite countertops, the black stone floor…they were covered with pots and skillets. Big ones. Small ones. Stainless steel. Ironware. Ceramic. The place was ankle-deep in cookware, more than he'd imagined he owned, because the stuff had all been the decorator's idea, not his.

Why would a man need a million things to cook in when he didn't cook?

In the center of it all was Chiara, dressed like an undertaker in a calf-length black something and clunky black shoes, her hair scraped back in that damned bun. Chiara, who had decided to take over his kitchen. Chiara, who was, without question, about to utter those famous eight words…

"What are you doing?" he said sharply.

She spun toward him. "Raffaele!"

"I asked you a question. What are you doing?"

She hesitated, looking around her, then at him. "I suppose you had no idea I could cook."

Okay. It was a variation but the theme was the same. Man, had he ever misjudged her!

She gave him a hesitant smile. "I was making coffee."

Rafe folded his arms over his chest. "Come on, baby." His voice was like ice. Amazing, considering that he could feel his blood pressure soaring into the stratosphere. "Just coffee? How about breakfast? Eggs. French toast. Waffles. You can make all that stuff, right?"

She swallowed. Nodded. Offered another cautious smile. Rafe could feel his anger growing. She wanted out of this marriage? The hell she did, he thought in escalating fury, and his BP went through the roof.

"I have a housekeeper," he snarled. "The time comes I want something cooked, I'll ask her to cook it."

Chiara's smile vanished. "Yes. Of course. I told you, I only wished to make coffee. Espresso. But I could not find an espresso pot so—"

"You couldn't find it because I don't have one. Or did you assume having an Italian name means I came out of my mother's womb with an espresso maker tucked in my…hands?"

"No. I mean, yes." She caught her lip between her teeth. "I did not mean to make you angry."

"I am not angry," Rafe said. "Why would I be

angry? Just because you've decided you don't want out of this nonsensical marriage—"

"What?"

"Just because you think the I-can-cook thing will change my mind—"

"You are *pazzo*! Of course I want—what did you call it—out of this marriage!" Her hands slapped on her hips. "And I have no idea what the I-can-cook thing is!"

"A likely story."

Chiara drew herself up. "I do not have to listen to this idiocy."

"No. You have to clean up my kitchen." Rafe glared. "Look at it. You tore it apart, and—"

The sound of something bubbling drew his attention. His gaze swept past her. His French press was on a front burner of the big Viking range. The burner glowed red-hot; the press was filled with water.

With boiling water.

He cursed, sprinted across the room, grabbed the French press and yelped when his fingers closed around the hot glass. The predictable thing happened. It slipped from his hands, smashed against the floor, and spewed hot water over his bare toes.

"Oh, *Dio mio!*"

Chiara threw out her hands. One connected with a cast-iron skillet. The predictable thing happened again. The skillet tumbled from the counter and landed on Rafe's still-naked, now scalded toes.

"Figlio di puttana!"

"Raffaele!" Chiara said, sounding shocked.

Rafe ignored her, hopped to the fridge and hit a button. Ice cubes tumbled into his hand. He squeezed his fingers around some, let the others dump on his toes.

Damn it all, his life had turned into a reality show. And it was all this woman's fault. No. It was his. Why had he brought her home with him? Okay, maybe he'd had to marry her. So what? He could have left her in Palermo. He could have dumped her at a Manhattan hotel. He could have done a hundred things that wouldn't have put her under his roof.

Chiara said his name again and he swung toward her.

"Are you…are you all right?"

"I'm fine," he said coldly.

She gestured at his hand, then at his foot. "I am sorry, Raffaele."

Her voice quavered. She was on the verge of tears. Who gave a damn?

"I only meant to do a good thing. To show you that I appreciate all you have done for me."

"The only way you could do that would be to erase yesterday, and that's not about to happen."

The tears appeared, filling her eyes until they glittered like diamonds. So what? Women were good at producing instant tears. It didn't change a thing.

"Stop that," he growled.

She turned her back and cried harder.

It made him feel bad but, hell, she probably wanted him to feel bad. She was clever. Somewhere between the ceremony in San Giuseppe and their arrival here, he'd managed to forget that. Well, he wouldn't forget it again. This was the woman who'd waylaid him on the road. Who'd kissed him as if she wanted to suck out his tonsils right before she went into her Petrified Virgin routine. Forget what he'd thought last night, that she was as much a victim as he was.

Still, he sure as hell didn't want her crying over a couple of stupid accidents.

"Okay," he said, "that's enough. It's only a kitchen."

"I burned your fingers."

"You didn't burn them, I did." He turned her toward him, held up his hand, flexed his fingers. "See? They're fine. That ice did the trick."

"I broke your toes."

"Toe. Just one. The big one." He looked down; so did she. He flexed his toes, forced himself not to wince. The damned thing probably was broken but he'd sooner have walked on nails that admit it. "See? It's fine. Ice can do wonders."

She gave a little hiccup and raised her face to his. Hell, he thought, his throat tightening, didn't they teach women how to sob delicately in Weeping 101 anymore? Because there was nothing delicate about Chiara's red eyes and runny nose. She was a veritable mess, as sorry a mess as the room and their marriage.

And yet she looked even more beautiful.

How could that be? Everything she had on was ugly. She wore no makeup. She'd wept her way into ruddy-faced disaster.

"Raffaele." Her voice broke. More tears overflowed and trickled down her cheeks. "I am so sorry. For everything. For ruining your life, ruining your kitchen—"

"Hush," he said, and then he did the only logical thing.

He cupped her face, brought his lips to hers and kissed her.

His head told him it was a mistake. You didn't kiss a woman you intended to get rid of. You certainly didn't kiss a woman who'd made it clear she was afraid of any kind of physical intimacy.

Except…except, she wasn't struggling. Wasn't gasping with fear or anger. No, he thought in wonder, no…

She was melting in his arms.

It happened so fast that it stunned him.

One second he was holding a weeping woman whose spine might have been fashioned of steel. The next, she was on her toes, leaning into him. Her arms were tight around his neck. Her heart was racing against his.

It was what should have happened early this morning, he thought…

And then he stopped thinking.

Her hands speared into his hair. She moaned, dragged his face down to hers. He whispered her name, slanted his mouth hungrily over hers, cupped her backside and lifted her up and into his straining erection. Her breath caught. He thought he'd frightened her but she moved against him, moved again, a tentative thrust of her lower body and it came as close as anything could to undoing him.

"Raffaele," she whispered.

The word trembled on her lips, wafted over his.

"Chiara. My beautiful Chiara."

His hands rose. Cupped her breasts. She cried out, said his name, made the sweet little sounds a woman makes when she wants a man.

He swept aside whatever remained on the granite counter, clasped her waist and lifted her onto it. *Not like this,* logic said, *not here, not for her first time!*

To hell with logic.

He wanted her, now. Needed her, now. He was dizzy with it, crazed with it, with wanting to kiss her, touch her, bury himself inside her.

Somehow he forced himself to slow down. He kissed her eyelids, her temples, her mouth. Sweet. Soft. Warm. Her lips clung to his. He felt the first delicate whisper of her tongue against his, and desire, hot and fierce, shot through him like an arrow.

"Raffaele? Raffaele. I want—I want—"

"Tell me," he said hoarsely, between deep, hot kisses. "Tell me what you want, sweetheart."

Everything, she thought. Oh *Dio*, she wanted everything.

Raffaele's mouth, drinking from hers. The silken intrusion of his tongue. His thumbs tracing the arc of her cheekbones, her throat, her breasts. And, yes, what he was doing now. Undoing the endless row of jet buttons on her dress. Baring her flesh to him. The curve of her breasts, rising above her bra.

He kissed the hollow of her throat. Nipped lightly at the skin. She gasped; her head fell back. She would have fallen back, too—she was boneless—but he caught her shoulders, his strong hands supporting her as he brought her to him and kissed her again and again.

It wasn't enough. None of it was enough. How could it be enough? She ached for him.

For his possession.

She sobbed his name. His eyes met hers. They were black with desire; the bones of his face stood out in stark relief.

She knew what it meant.

For the first time, a frisson of fear slid greasily through her belly.

"Raffaele," she said breathlessly, "Raffaele…"

He grasped the hem of her dress, bunched it in

his big hands and raised it to the tops of her thighs. Stepped between them. Still watching her face, he laid one hand over that place between her legs, that temple of evil her mother had warned against.

She cried out.

"Raffaele," she said, and he slipped his fingers under the edge of her underpants, and now she felt the wetness in that place, the heat, the throbbing of her pulse…

"Omylord," a woman's voice squealed. "Oh, Mr. Orsini! I had no idea—"

Chiara froze. Rafe went still.

"I'll come back later, sir, shall I? Of course. That's what I'll do. I'm so sorry, sir…"

A low moan rose in Chiara's throat. She shot into motion, a blur of energy as she jumped from the counter, then tried to fight free of Rafe's arms as they swept around her.

"Easy," he whispered.

She struggled against him but he refused to let go. She was saying something in Sicilian, saying it again and again in a low, anguished voice.

He thought it might be that she wanted to die, and his heart turned over.

"Chiara."

She shook her head. Her eyes were screwed tightly shut, like a child's, as if what she couldn't see couldn't hurt her.

"Sweetheart. Look at me."

Another shake of her head. Rafe sighed, brought her face against his shoulder. For all her offer to leave and return later, his housekeeper was still standing in the entrance to the kitchen, her eyes as round as her face, one hand plastered over her heart.

Rafe cleared his throat. "Good morning, Mrs. O'Hara," he said pleasantly.

The woman bobbed her head. "Morning, Mr. Orsini. I am terribly sorry. I never meant—"

"No, of course you didn't."

He looked from his housekeeper to the woman in his arms. There were simple choices here. He could let Chiara go. She'd bolt and run and probably add this to her already distorted ideas of sex.

Or he could hold on to her while he played the scene through. It was, after all, only a minor embarrassment. Someone stumbling across a man and woman about to have sex? There was nothing original about it. Told in the right company, it would prove amusing.

He could feel Chiara trembling against him, her tears soaking his sweater.

Rafe paused. In his twenties, he'd gone bungee jumping. He remembered how it had felt, that gut-wrenching moment when he'd been about to jump off the bridge railing into the there's-no-turning-back void.

"Mrs. O'Hara," he said, "Mrs. O'Hara...I'd like to introduce you to my wife."

CHAPTER NINE

IF YOU were an anthropologist doing field work, you might have put The Bar on a threatened-species list.

No rope at the door to keep out those who might offend the fashionistas. No VIP lists. No hot babes in spandex, no guys with more money than brains, no drinks with names that made a man laugh.

In fact, the place was so low-key that you had to know it existed before you could find it. Wood-paneled, dimly lit, it was located in an un-remarkable Soho neighborhood. At least, it had been unremarkable when the Orsini brothers had discovered it years ago.

They'd been just starting out back then, three of them with unused degrees in finance and business in their pockets and one, Falco, with enough university credits for a couple of degrees but not enough concentration in any one area to matter. They'd all turned their backs on the white-collar world. Cesare, sneering, said it was to find themselves.

The truth was, they'd gone off to lose their connection to everything he represented.

Rafe and Nick had ended up in the military, one in the Marines, one in the Army, both fighting wars neither wanted to talk about. Falco was even more tight-lipped about his time in Special Forces. Dante had headed north to Alaska and the dangers of the oil fields on the North Slope. He and Falco were the only ones who'd returned with money in their pockets, Dante from his job, Falco from the high-stakes poker games he loved.

Dante, Nick and Rafe had quickly figured out that they wanted to build a future together. Falco wasn't sure what he wanted.

They began getting together a couple of nights a week at a place called O'Hearn's Bar. It was a neighborhood place, located just downstairs from Rafe's one-room-with-what-passed-for-a-kitchen walkup. The beer was cold, the sandwiches were cheap, and nobody gave a damn who the brothers were.

Gradually the last booth on the left became known as theirs. It was where they met and discussed Life and Women and What To Do with Their Lives.

Eventually they figured out a way to combine their talents, temperaments and education. Rafe and Nick pooled their resources, played what was then a booming stock market, put the money into the new venture. Dante added his impressive oil field savings. Six months later Falco decided to throw in his luck with his brothers and put them over the top with the not-so-small fortune he'd made at poker.

Orsini Brothers was born.

Their corporate baby flourished. So did the neighborhood around O'Hearn's. Tired old tenements, including the one where Rafe had lived, were gutted and reborn as pricey town houses. A factory building became a high-priced club. Bodegas became boutiques.

The Orsinis could tell that O'Hearn's days were numbered.

"We've got to do something," Falco had grumbled, so they did. They bought the place, and it became the smallest and least noticed part of the Orsini Brothers' holdings.

They cleaned it up, but only a little. Had the planked oak floor refinished. Tore out the worn leather stools and banquettes and replaced them with new ones. Everything else—the scarred wood tables, the pressed-tin ceiling, the long zinc counter, the beers on draught, the over-stuffed sandwiches and killer grilled-with-onions burgers—stayed the same.

To the brothers' shock, O'Hearn's Bar—by now, simply known as The Bar—became what people referred to as a "destination." Still, only the bartenders knew who owned it, and that was exactly how the Orsinis wanted it.

That way they could avoid the reporters from the *Times* and the *Wall Street Journal* as well as the ones from the tabloids. It wasn't easy to keep your privacy when you'd created a company worth billions—and your old man was still *numero uno* whenever some damned investigative reporter dredged up the *M* word.

So, The Bar was the logical place to get together every couple of Friday nights, or maybe after closing on Saturday night if a date had proved especially memorable. It was also where you went if you just wanted to talk.

Like today.

Falco and Nick, back from their business meetings overseas, were already there when

Rafe arrived. Only Dante was missing. He was off somewhere in South America. Nobody knew where or why. Rafe figured it had something to do with that Sunday morning meeting with Cesare but decided it was Dante's business to talk about it, not his.

He sure as hell wasn't going to say anything about what had happened at *his* Sunday morning meeting with his father…and if he wasn't, what was he doing here? he thought, as he stepped from the sunlight into The Bar's artificial gloom.

He'd phoned Nick and Falco on the spur of the moment. They'd both been at work, as he should have been, when he called. "Got time for a beer?" he'd said, and they'd said sure.

Now, seeing them, his gut knotted.

Why he'd suggested getting together was beyond him. He had a problem on his hands but he wasn't about to lay it out for discussion. There was still time to turn around and walk away—but Nick looked up, spotted him and it was too late.

Nothing to do now but fake some casual conversation. Rafe fixed what he hoped was a smile on his face, sauntered over to their usual booth and slid in beside Falco.

"Hey."

"Hey."

So much for casual conversation.

The bartender, who'd spotted Rafe the second he walked in, came over with an icy mug of ale. Rafe nodded his thanks. His brothers watched as he took a long swallow.

"Well," he said brightly, "it's good to see you guys."

Nick looked at Falco. "At least he doesn't look as bad as he sounded."

And so much for getting through this un-scathed. Rafe concentrated on his mug of beer.

Falco shrugged. "He looks worse."

Okay. Enough. Rafe looked up.

"I am," he said, "right here. No reason to talk as if I weren't."

"Sure." Nick nodded agreeably. "No reason not to tell you, to your face, that Falco's right. You look like *caca*."

"Thank you."

"You want compliments, you're in the wrong place," Falco said, but his usually hard expression softened. A bad sign, Rafe thought glumly. "So, you want to tell us what's going on?"

Rafe thought of making another clever response, but what was the point? His brothers knew him too well to be fooled. Besides, he was the idiot who'd called this meeting and brought this on his own head.

"Nothing. It's just been a long couple of days."

Nick raised his eyebrows. "That's it?"

Another shrug. Another swallow of beer. Then Rafe pressed the icy bottle against his temple, where a Chinese orchestra playing traditional Mandarin melodies had moved in to replace the departed trolls.

"I, ah, I have some things to sort out."

"Such as?" Nick asked.

"Just…things."

Nick looked at Falco. "Your turn."

Falco scowled. Nobody could scowl quite like Falco.

"You want to tell us what's happening? You don't show up at the office—"

"I'm entitled to a day off," Rafe said, trying not to sound defensive.

"You don't show up," Falco continued, "then you phone us and say you need to talk—"

"I never said that."

"You didn't have to. It's Monday, the market's in the toilet and here we are, taking a break at your request. You really think we're going to think it's just so we could all say 'hello, what's new, how was your weekend?'"

"Hello," Rafe said, "what's new, how was your—" A muscle knotted in his jaw. "Okay. It's true. I have a, uh, a slight problem."

"Blonde or brunette?"

"That's insulting, Nicolo. I mean, why jump to the conclusion that it's a female problem?"

"Blonde or brunette," Nick repeated, and Rafe sighed.

"Brunette."

"What happened to the Valkyrie?"

"She's history."

"How come?"

Rafe narrowed his eyes. "Are we going to discuss the past or the current situation?"

"Don't get testy," Falco said mildly. "Okay. So, what *is* the current situation?"

Rafe stared at his brothers. The thing was, he *did* know why he'd phoned them. Who else would he turn to when he was in a mess straight up to his eyeballs? And, damn it, yes, this thing was a mess.

He was married. Married, him, a man who'd never even contemplated marriage, who'd run like hell anytime a woman so much as breathed the word. He was married to a stranger from a world so unlike his it would have been funny if it hadn't been so unbelievable.

That was item one in the "current situation."

Item two was that even though he was going to end the marriage as quickly as he could pull it off, that hadn't kept him from, item three, damned near making it with Chiara on his kitchen counter, which led, inexorably, to item four, that she was almost certainly a virgin and having sex with her would, oh damn, item five, make ending the marriage more complicated, never mind item six, that he'd introduced her as his wife and she wasn't, well, she was, legally, and—

"Rafe?"

And what a disaster of a scene that had been. His housekeeper had all but burst into congratulatory song. Not Chiara. She'd turned bright pink.

"I am *not* your wife," she'd said, "and if you think that—that assaulting me makes it so, you are wrong!"

Then she'd fled.

He'd thought about trying to explain things to his housekeeper—who'd gone from looking at him through misty eyes to regarding him as if he'd turned into a serial killer right in front of her—given that up and gone after Chiara instead, but she'd locked her door and when he'd tried to talk to her—

"Raffaele!"

Rafe's head came up. "Why'd you call me that?" he said, glaring at Nick.

"Because it's your name. Because you're a thousand miles away. Because one of us is nuts and the odds are excellent I'm looking at him. What's the brunette's name?"

Mrs. Orsini, Rafe thought wildly, and choked back what began as an insane cackle.

"This is amusing?"

"No," Rafe said quickly, "believe me, it isn't."

"So, what's the lady's name?"

"Chiara."

Falco raised an eyebrow. "Very nice. Very sexy."

"She isn't."

"Nice? Or very sexy?"

"She's not like that, is what I'm saying. She's, ah, she's different."

"They're always different," Falco said, "until they get to feeling comfortable." He made interlocking damp rings on the beat-up tabletop with his beer mug. "I take it this one isn't feeling comfortable yet."

Comfortable? A muscle tightened in Rafe's jaw. She was living in his apartment. Somehow he didn't want to admit that. He didn't want to admit anything. He wished to God he'd never started this conversation. In another few minutes his brothers would go from calling him nuts to figuring he needed to be committed.

"Okay," Falco said, "I get it. You got involved on the rebound. Now you want out. You do, don't you? Want out? I mean, that's what this is all about?"

Rafe nodded. "Absolutely."

"I don't see the problem. Take the lady to dinner. You know, the it's-been-great-but-it's-over meal."

"It isn't like that. She wants out, too."

Nick stared at him. "Well, then there isn't any problem."

"There is." Rafe hesitated. "It's…it's compli-cated. I mean, we both want out. But—"

"But?"

"But, she's, ah, she's new to the city."

"Buy her a guidebook," Falco said coldly.

"And, ah, and I came on to her and that, ah, that kind of upset her."

Falco and Nick grinned at each other. "So much for those smooth Orsini moves," Nick said.

"Hey, I'm trying to be serious here. What I mean is… See, the lady in question is a little wary. Of men. Of sex. Of me. And, uh, and now I'm wondering if I…if I—" He swallowed hard. "She won't talk to me."

This time nobody grinned. "She's frigid?" Falco said, his eyebrows aiming for his hairline.

"No. Yes. I mean, maybe. I mean, it doesn't matter because I have no intention of keeping her around very long."

His brothers were looking at him strangely. He couldn't blame them.

"Back to what Falco suggested," Nick said. "Dinner. She won't talk to you? No problem. Leave a message on her voice mail. Tell her to meet you somewhere for dinner. When she shows up, tell her things aren't working. Give her a little gift, you know, not the little-blue-box-from-Tiffany's kind of thing, but… What? Why are you shaking your head?"

"No phone. No voice mail." Rafe cleared his throat. "She's living in my apartment."

The look of incredulity on his brothers' faces said it all.

"She's—"

"—living with you?"

"It's temporary."

"You sent the Valkyrie packing a couple of days ago and moved this Clara—"

"Chiara."

"Clara, Chiara, whatever. You moved her in, what, five minutes later?"

Rafe gave one last thought to explaining, but how could he, when not even he could make sense out of everything he'd done? The only certainty was that he'd gotten himself into this mess and it was up to him to get himself out of it.

"Hey," he said brightly, after a glance at his watch, "look at the time!"

"Rafe. Wait a minute—"

But he was already on his feet. "Great seeing you guys," he said, and scrambled for the door.

Nick and Falco watched him go. Then they looked at each other.

"You got any idea what just happened?" Nick said.

Falco shook his head. "Not in the slightest."

Nick nodded and signaled for another round of beer.

Rafe had taxied downtown.

His condo was on Fifth Avenue, in the midsixties. Any way you looked at it, it was a long walk home, but that was a good thing. Long walks usually helped clear his head.

Involving his brothers had not been a good idea. Not that he'd really involved them. He hadn't told them much of anything, but what he had told them was not good.

Still, the confrontation, if you could call it that, had had one positive effect. It had made him face reality. He'd been dealing with this as if he were standing outside the problem, observing it. He wasn't. What he was, he thought as he passed a group of suburban women in for some shopping and dressed more for a New Jersey mall than for the eclectic streets of Soho, what he was, was a man standing in a hole six feet deep, busy digging himself in deeper.

He'd married Chiara, yes, but given the same circumstances, he'd have done it again. What kind of man would turn his back on a desperate woman? And it wasn't because of how she looked, those big violet eyes, that trembling mouth, or of how that mouth had felt under his, or of how she'd felt in his arms.

She'd needed help. He'd offered it. So, okay. The marrying part had been necessary.

What had been going on since then was not. The arguing. The accusations. What was the point? It was a done deal. And then, this morning… Proof of how crazy things had gotten. He couldn't imagine why he'd tried to jump her bones.

To say she wasn't his type was a laugh. She had a pretty face, yeah, but so did a million other women, and none of those million other women went around looking like little old ladies. None of them would ever look at him as if he were a mustachioed villain.

None of them was a wife he didn't want. And none of them had hang-ups about sex.

Not that Chiara had seemed to have many of those this morning. That kiss. The way she'd clung to him. Moaned into his mouth. Arched her body against his, lifted herself to him…

Just what he needed. Turning himself on while he walked down a crowded street. Oh, yes, that was a great idea.

He swung toward a shop window, found himself staring at a display of hammers and power tools while he fought for control. That was another thing. When had he ever had to struggle for self-control? Never. Not since he'd left the Marines. Now he fought for it all the time. Either he was furious at his wife or so turned on that he couldn't see straight for wanting her and—

"And she isn't your wife," he said sharply.

A couple coming out of the store gave him a wary look.

"Sorry," Rafe said, "sorry. I was just—"

He was just losing his mind. The couple moved quickly past him. He took some deep breaths, began walking again.

It was time to move on. She wanted a divorce. So did he. He pulled his cell phone from his pocket as he reached the corner. The light turned red. Time to separate the tourists from the natives. The tourists stayed on the curb. The New Yorkers, Rafe among them, kept going. A car horn bleeped. A voice shouted something. Rafe met the driver's eyes, flashed a look that silenced him.

Rafe stepped onto the curb, brought up his contact list, selected Marilyn Sayers's number. Her phone rang and rang. When it finally picked up, what he got was not her but her voice mail.

"Marilyn," he said impatiently, "it's Rafe Orsini. Pick up if you're there. Or call me back, fast. It's urgent."

He'd hardly closed the phone when it rang.

He glanced at the face plate, saw with relief that it was her.

"Marilyn. Thanks for getting back to me so fast. No, I'm okay. I'm just in a messy situation, is all. See—" She interrupted. He blinked. "You're where?"

She was in Istanbul. Five thousand miles away. Something about the first vacation she and her husband had taken in years, blah-blah-blah, but Rafe didn't give a damn. All that registered was that she'd be gone another week.

"A week?" He shook his head as he navigated a particularly crowded stretch of Sixth Avenue. "Impossible. I have a problem. A personal problem. And— Marilyn?"

The call broke up, then died. Rafe cursed, hit redial. Marilyn picked up and said they had a bad connection.

"Yeah. I know. Listen, this problem I have—"

She interrupted again, told him to get in touch with her partner. He'd handle things. Rafe shook his head, as if she could see him. Sayers's partner was ninety if he was a day, a starchy old guy who wore a vest, carried a pocket watch and took ten years to shuffle across a room.

Explain to him how he'd come to have a wife

who wasn't a wife? Ask him to expedite things so they could get divorced quickly because if they spent another day together, he was liable to strip his wife-who-wasn't-a-wife out of her ugly black clothes and bare all her soft, sweet flesh to his eyes and hands and mouth?

"No good," he growled. "I need you, not your partner."

It was useless. Sayers was sorry but— The line went dead. Rafe snarled and closed the phone with a vengeful snap.

Okay. What now? Easy. Get Chiara out from under his roof. A week's wait was nothing, once he'd done that. Out of sight, out of mind.

He'd find her a place to live. It was an excellent idea, one that would bolster the fact that the marriage wasn't a marriage at all. And how hard could it be to find someplace to stash her? The city was loaded with real estate agents. He just needed one who'd move his request to the top of the list.

Of course!

Rafe flipped the phone open, checked his contact list again, hit a button.

"Chilton Realtors."

"Elaine Chilton, please."

It was the perfect solution. Why deal with an

agent he didn't know when he had one at his fingertips? He'd met the Chilton woman somewhere. A party, a dinner. It didn't matter. She'd tugged his phone from his hand after he'd taken a call, smiled prettily and programmed in her number.

"In case you ever need me," she'd purred.

He hadn't. He'd been involved with Ingrid at the time but he sure as hell needed her now.

"Hello?"

"Elaine? It's Rafe Orsini."

"Well, well, well," she said in a throaty whisper, "how are you, Mr. Orsini?"

He said he was fine and then he cut to the chase, said he was interested in seeing her.

"It's urgent," he said.

She gave a sexy little laugh. "How nice!"

Rafe felt a second's unease. Were they talking about the same thing?

"Where are you?" she asked.

He told her.

"Perfect. I have a rental a couple of blocks away."

"What's it like?"

Another little laugh. "I'm sure you'll think it's perfect." She gave him the address, told him to meet her there in twenty minutes.

Rafe disconnected, his concerns gone. Perfect?

Absolutely. He checked his watch, turned down Fifty-seventh Street…

Half an hour later, he was striding towards his condo, furious at fate, at life, at his own stupidity.

Elaine Chilton had been waiting for him, all right…on a pale pink sofa in a red silk teddy and black stilettos, and okay, maybe he hadn't handled things exactly right. Maybe you didn't look at a half-naked woman and say, "Oh sorry! See, what I meant was, I'm interested in finding an apartment for this woman who's living with me."

Definitely a poor choice of words, he thought as he marched into his own apartment building, glowered at the hapless doorman and stepped into his elevator.

He probably deserved the names the Chilton babe had called him, if not the slap. At least he'd stopped himself from saying, "Okay, now that that's out of the way, what about the rental?"

The car shot upward. Next step was to call a hotel. The Waldorf. The St. Regis. Not as homey as a furnished apartment but who cared? What counted was that Chiara would be there, he would be here. And as soon as Sayers was in her office, things would start to be okay.

The elevator door slid open. Rafe stepped out—and found Chiara, waiting for him as Elaine Chilton had been waiting.

Not quite.

No silk teddy. No stiletto heels. No pink sofa. Chiara was seated in his foyer in an Eames chair, back straight, knees all but locked, hands folded in her lap, dressed in yet another of those incredibly ugly black outfits.

Then, why did seeing her go through him like a surge of electricity?

"Raffaele." She rose to her feet, hands still tightly clasped. "I am sorry."

Her voice was small but her eyes were steady on his. She was that combination of vulnerability and defiance that got to him every time.

"I seem to say that to you a great deal but…" She licked her lips. He could no more have kept from following the quick swipe of her pink tongue than he could have kept from breathing. "But I overreacted. You were simply trying to save me from embarrassment in front of your housekeeper. I should have understood that."

Rafe forced his gaze from her mouth. Not a good plan. He looked into her eyes, instead, and saw that they glittered with unshed tears.

"No," he said, "it's my fault. I've handled this all wrong. I know what you want and I—" Why was his voice so rough? He cleared his throat. "I've been in touch with my attorney."

Chiara shook her head. Her hair was still loose. He'd set it free hours ago, when he'd kissed her. The wildness of her curls was in direct contrast to her black dress and sensible shoes.

"Please, let me finish. This is difficult for me but I must say it." She drew a deep breath. "The…the kissing, Raffaele. It was inexcusable."

"Yes." He swiped his hand through his hair. "I'm sorry about that, Chiara. I shouldn't have—"

"My response, I mean. It was wrong. I have no explanation to offer. I can only say I regret it and—"

"Don't," he said quickly, his voice even rougher. "Don't regret it, sweetheart. Please."

"But I…" Color flooded her face. "I should not have kissed you back."

"Chiara. That was a good thing. A healthy thing. Responding to a man's kisses. To *my* kisses."

"But I do not… I have never…"

Her voice faded. She looked away from him. She'd known this would be difficult, admitting that what happened whenever he touched her was as much her fault as his, but what she hadn't expected was that seeing him would make her feel light-headed. Almost dizzy. Afraid to keep meeting his gaze because looking into his beautiful blue eyes made her want to…want to…

She felt a light touch on her hair. His hand, stroking the curls back from her temples. His fingers, threading into the strands. A moan rose in her throat. What was happening? She wanted to sigh his name, lift her face to his…

"No," she said quickly, "no, it must not happen again. Those things I did—"

"You kissed me," he said in a low voice. "And I kissed you. Kissing isn't wrong, sweetheart."

Somehow, his hand was cupping her chin. Somehow, her face was lifting to his.

And then his mouth was on hers.

He was kissing her, kissing her gently, and she was kissing him back. She caught his sweater in her hands, knotted the soft cotton in her fists and rose to him.

His arms swept around her. He gathered her against him and she framed his face with her hands, her lips soft and warm against his. She was making little sounds, moans of pleasure and desire, and he knew she was his for the taking.

He had only to lift her into his arms, carry her up the stairs to his bed. What he wanted, what he had wanted from the first time he'd kissed her, would become reality.

He would make love to her.

Take her innocence.

Take it, and be no better than bastards like her father and Giglio, men who would exploit this beautiful, brave woman instead of honoring and protecting her.

He kissed her one last time. Then he rested his forehead against hers.

"Chiara." His voice sounded rusty; he cleared his throat. "Sweetheart. I have a great idea. Let's…let's start over."

"Start over?"

"Yes. You. Me. The situation we're in… We don't have to be enemies, Chiara. We can be friends."

She looked baffled. Why wouldn't she? It was probably the last thing she'd expected him to say. Hell, it was the last thing *he'd* expected to say. But it was right, and he knew it.

He would be her friend, not her lover, even if it killed him.

"I would like that," she said softly. "To start over with you, Raffaele."

Then she smiled, and he wondered how it was possible for everything good in the world to be captured in a woman's smile.

CHAPTER TEN

HE KNEW he had to get the two of them out of his apartment.

He was a man, not a martyr. All his good intentions could easily come undone if this sweet, intimate moment stretched on. So he flashed a quick smile, let go of her and stepped back.

"I," he said briskly, "am hungry enough to eat a bear."

She laughed. "I think it would be difficult to find a bear on Fifth Avenue."

"Oh, I don't know. This is a pretty amazing city."

Chiara nodded. "I have read that it is."

She had read about New York. Read about it, but not seen it. He'd been so wrapped up in his own selfish misery he hadn't given a thought to what might make things easier for her.

She'd just given him the answer.

He could show her his town. And in the process keep her at a safe distance. A win-win situation, he thought, and decided not to waste time. He took her hand, hurried her to the elevator. When she asked where they were going, he grinned and said they were in pursuit of that bear.

Of course, none of the restaurants he had in mind had bear on the menu, but he had a long list of favorite places. They'd all be jammed this time of day, but that wasn't a problem. He'd never needed a reservation to get a great table. It was one of the benefits of being Rafe Orsini.

When they reached the lobby and he asked the doorman to flag a taxi, Chiara held back.

Rafe looked at her. "What?"

"Nothing. Nothing at all."

Not true. Something was troubling her; she was biting gently on her bottom lip, the way she always did when she was upset, and if he kept watching her do it he was going to scoop her into his arms and ravish her, right here. The hot image made him sound brusque.

"Chiara, look, if you don't want to do this—"

"Oh, no, Raffaele." She put her hand lightly on his arm. "I just wondered…could we take the subway?"

"The what?"

"The subway. I have read about it. It is in the

ground. Well, most of it is in the ground. It whisks people through the city, from one borough to another, from Bronx all the way to the end of the Brooklyn. *Sì?*"

She sounded like a tour guide. He wanted to haul her into his arms and kiss her.

"*Sì,*" Rafe said, smiling. "But it's *the* Bronx, and just plain Brooklyn.

"Ah. I see. But it is probably foolish…"

Foolish? That his wife would prefer to ride the subway instead of a taxi? Rafe smiled and took her hand.

"It's a great idea," he said. "I should have thought of it."

He warned her it was a few blocks' walk to the nearest subway station. She smiled and told him she loved to walk. He had never known a woman who said that and meant it, but his Chiara did. She craned her neck at the skyscrapers, gaped at the shop windows, almost skipped along the crowded sidewalks.

"Oh," she said, eyes shining, "I have never seen anything like this!"

No, he thought, watching her. Neither had he.

Rockefeller Center, when they finally reached it, rated a huge gasp.

"The statue of Prometheus!"

Well, hell, was that the name of the big gilded guy? Rafe hadn't known that. Chiara told him all about it. The legend. The sculptor. How the statue had come to be placed here. He listened, but mostly he just heard his wife's voice. Soft. Silvery. Happy.

That was the word.

She was happy.

So was he.

He had never been so happy in his life, he thought in amazement, and while she was still bubbling about Prometheus, he swung her into his arms and kissed her, right there in Rockefeller Center surrounded by thousands of people. Nobody seemed to notice. This was, after all, New York. But when he finally took his lips from hers and she opened her eyes and he saw how they were glowing, he thought he might be more than happy, that he was—that he was—

"Hungry," he said, the word coming out quick and sharp, as if he were a man just realizing he'd stepped back from the edge of a cliff. "Why don't we, ah, why don't we get something to eat?"

His head was spinning. He couldn't think

straight. What was nearby? Where could he take her that she would enjoy? Because that was what this was all about, wasn't it? Showing his wife—this temporary wife—his city? She was his guest. She'd never been to New York before; for all he knew, after their divorce, she might choose to return to Italy.

No. Damn it, no. She wouldn't do that. Go all the way across the ocean. Go so far away from him…

Somebody bumped into them. Rafe blinked, clasped Chiara's hand and set off at brisk pace.

La Grenouille.

That was the name of the restaurant he took her to.

Chiara knew it meant frog, though why anyone would name a place so elegant after so humble a creature was beyond her.

She also understood what Raffaele did not.

She was as out of place here as, well, as a frog.

Everyone was looking at her. Okay. Maybe not everyone, but they might as well have been. The diners were as upscale as the restaurant, the women all fashionably dressed, their faces and hair testament to time spent in the city's finest salons.

What must they think of her in her ugly black dress, ugly black shoes, ugly black coat? Not that it mattered. Her Raffaele was an amazing man, but he would never get a table here. It was too crowded. And then there was the way she looked…

But they did get a table. Immediately. A banquette, and she knew, instinctively, it was a coveted spot. Waiters appeared. Busboys. Menus, wine lists…

She told Raffaele to order for her.

It was enough to watch him select a wine, a meal, to watch him smile when she bit into her salmon and offered a sigh of approval.

And it was more than enough to watch the women watching him, their covetous glances turning to disbelief when they turned their attention to her.

Yes, she thought, her chin lifting, oh, yes, I am with this man. This beautiful man who is generous and kind and caring.

Was that why the waitstaff deferred to him? Or was it because of something darker? Was her Raffaele's power similar to that of her father?

Chiara's meal, until now so perfect, suddenly seemed inedible.

"Chiara?"

She looked up. Raffaele was watching her. He looked troubled.

"Sweetheart, if you don't like what I ordered for you—"

"No. No, it is fine. I am…I am tired, I think. All that walking…"

He was on his feet in a second, helping her from her chair, dropping a stack of bills on the table. The captain hurried toward them. Was everything all right?

No, Chiara thought, everything was not all right. She was married to a man who was everything she despised…except, she was not really married to him and she did not really despise him. What she felt for him was— It was—

A tremor went through her. Raffaele curved his arm around her.

"I'll get a taxi," he said softly, "and we'll go home."

She nodded. Except, it wasn't her home, it was his. This was all temporary. And that was good, was it not? Of course it was. She had no place in Raffaele Orsini's life. She didn't want a place in it. She didn't, didn't, didn't…

Oh, God.

She did.

* * *

When they reached his place, he wanted to call his doctor.

Chiara refused. She was still pale but at least she had stopped trembling.

"I am tired, Raffaele, that is all. A night's sleep and I'll be fine."

She went to her room. He went out to his. It was still early. He thought about phoning Falco. Or Nicolo. Thought about opening his BlackBerry and phoning a woman. The one he'd met the night he'd ended things with Ingrid…

Instead, he undressed, put on a pair of sweats and turned on the TV. Watched an old football game on ESPN. An even older movie on HBO. Clicked through the zillion channels that had absolutely nothing worth viewing and finally tossed the damned remote aside in disgust.

Taking Chiara out today had been a stupid idea.

She wasn't his guest any more than she was his wife. She was an encumbrance. A beautiful encumbrance, but that didn't change a thing. The sooner he called Sayers's law partner, the better. He'd get a couple of hours' sleep and do it first thing in the morning.

But he couldn't sleep. Just as well because

somewhere around dawn he got an idea. A really good one.

He had that place on Nantucket. Why not put it to good use? Phone the couple who looked after it when he wasn't there, tell them to prepare for a guest, arrange for the helicopter service he occasionally used to fly Chiara to the island.

Brilliant, he thought as he showered and dressed, then went down the hall to her room and knocked on the door. She would be there. He would be here. No more nonsense, no more temptation—

The door swung open. Rafe stared at his wife. She was wearing another ugly outfit, her face was, as always, bare of makeup, her hair was loose and wild, still damp from the shower.

"Raffaele," she said shakily, "I am so sorry I spoiled our evening…"

Rafe groaned, hauled her into his arms and kissed her, and when she rose on her toes and kissed him back, he knew there wasn't a way in the world he was going to send her anywhere.

"Baby," he said gruffly, "you don't owe me an apology."

"Yes. I do. I thought—I suddenly thought that all this made no sense. You. Me. Our marriage…"

Who you are.

The words ran through her mind but she didn't speak them. For now, it was enough to know who her Raffaele seemed to be.

A man in whose arms she felt safe and wanted.

For as long as it lasted, she would not think of anything more than that.

They had breakfast.

She cooked. Bacon. Eggs. Toast. He ate it all, every bite, and never once thought about the grapefruits languishing in the refrigerator. But he made the coffee, teasing her about it until she laughed and said he had to buy an espresso pot and she would show him how to make real coffee.

Then they went out to see the city. Because, Rafe decided, what was the sense in asking Sayers's partner to start the ball rolling? Surely, waiting another few days wouldn't be a problem.

They rode the subway. Up to the Bronx, out to the end of the line in Brooklyn. It was a warm day. They strolled the boardwalk at Coney Island. The rides were closed, but Rafe told Chiara what the big amusement park was like when it was open, what it had been like years ago when he and his brothers had played hooky a couple of times and spent the day here.

"Hooky?"

"Yeah. You know. Cut school."

She didn't understand that, either, so he explained. It made her laugh.

"A couple of times, huh?"

He grinned and said, well, yeah, just a couple of times. The other times, they'd gone to other places.

He told her about Dante. And Nicolo. And Falco. She said, wistfully, that it must have been nice, growing up with brothers. He said there were times they were a pain in the—in the behind but that mostly they were great guys.

Around noon he suggested they head back to Manhattan to have lunch.

Chiara cast a longing look at Nathan's hot dog stand.

"I do not suppose," she said, "I do not imagine you would prefer to have—"

"Hot dogs?" Rafe laughed, picked her up, swung in a circle with her while she tried to keep a serious face as she demanded he put her down. "A kiss, and I will," he said, and letting her go after that one modest peck on the lips was the hardest thing he'd ever done.

They went into Nathan's. He ordered his hot

dog with mustard. She ordered hers with sauer-kraut. And onions. And relish.

"May I have French fries, too, please, Raffaele?"

He wanted to tell her she could have anything she wanted, that she already had—that she already had—

"Fries," he told the kid behind the counter, and told himself to stop thinking, because wherever his head was taking him made absolutely no sense at all.

He'd heard people say that seeing the city with someone who'd never seen it before was eye opening.

Seeing it with his Chiara was more than that. It was wonderful. It was amazing. It was incredible.

It was agony.

The days flew by, and he knew they were living on borrowed time. No matter how many places he showed her, how many little parks and mews they explored, no matter how many chestnut vendors his wife charmed by telling them their chestnuts were perfectly roasted, this was all going to end, and soon.

A good thing, of course. He had his life to lead.

That he hadn't gone to the office in days, that he had no desire to go to it, well, that was not good.

Neither was taking so many cold showers.

What choice did he have? A man walked a beautiful woman to the door of her room every night, kissed her, told himself the kiss would be on the cheek or on the forehead and, instead, ended up capturing her lips with his, ended up with her arms wound tightly around his neck and her sweet, lush body pressed to his…

A man had that happening to him, the only way to save his ass was to stumble down the hall and step into a long, icy shower. Well, if that was the price he had to pay for hours of laughter and companionship—companionship with a woman!—he'd pay it.

The truth was, he loved everything they did. Going to the museums. Walking in the park. Even riding the upper deck of a sightseeing bus. He'd felt like a jerk at first. Then his Chiara had turned her shining, excited face to his and he'd gone from feeling stupid to feeling like a lucky man.

The one thing they hadn't done, the one thing he longed to do, was buy his wife new clothes to replace those awful things she kept pulling out of her seemingly bottomless suitcase.

But he wasn't a fool. His Chiara was proud. If he so much as suggested buying her new stuff, he knew he might hurt her. And he'd sooner have slit his throat than do that. Besides, she was beautiful to him just as she was and anytime he caught some idiot looking at her and smirking, Rafe turned the smirk to panic with one cold glance.

So, the days were perfect. But there was, inevitably, that time each evening he left Chiara at her bedroom door.

He was a healthy, heterosexual male with healthy appetites. He'd wanted a lot of women in his life...but he had never wanted one the way he wanted her. His body ached for her. Well, why wouldn't it?

The problem was, his heart ached, too.

Crazy, he knew, because sex and desire had nothing to do with the heart.

That was what he was busy telling himself at the end of yet another long day. They'd had fun but without warning, over dinner at a little place in Chinatown, somewhere between the steamed dumplings and the Szechuan beef, Rafe looked at his wife and that aching heart of his suddenly hardened.

What kind of game was she playing?

This was her fault. All of it. That they were married. That they were in this mess. That he was going crazy, torn between wanting to drag her into his bed and believing he had to treat her as if she were made of glass.

And she knew it. Women always knew these things.

What did it all mean? Was it an act? The country mouse bit. The give-me-the-simple-life thing. The hot kisses that she had to know ended for him in the kind of anguish he hadn't experienced since he was sixteen.

Was it an act?

What else could it be? he thought coldly. And while she was in the middle of saying something about something—who gave a damn what—he tossed his chopsticks on his plate and got to his feet.

Chiara looked up. "Raffaele?"

"It's late," he said gruffly. "And I'm going back to work tomorrow." He hadn't known that until he said it, but, by God, it was one damned fine idea. He yanked out his wallet, tossed some bills on the table. "Let's go."

She was staring at him. He didn't blink, not

even when her eyes began to glitter. Not tears, he told himself. A trick of the light. Or maybe a trick of hers.

"Let's go," he repeated, and she put down her chopsticks and stood up.

By the time they got a taxi, she was crying. Silently, but she was crying. Was she upset because he'd pulled aside the curtain and taken a good look at what was behind it?

Frankly, he didn't care. This was it. No more. Sayers would be back tomorrow. Perfect timing. He'd phone her, set the divorce in motion, and that would be that.

They rode the taxi in silence, took the elevator to his place the same way. Was she still crying? He couldn't tell. Her head was turned away; her dark hair hid her face. Good. He'd looked at that face once too often.

When they stepped into the foyer of his penthouse, she swung toward him.

"Raffaele." Her voice trembled. Resolutely he folded his arms over his chest. "Raffaele. What did I do?"

"Nothing," he said calmly. "I'm the one. I should have dealt with reality sooner. We're nothing to each other, Chiara, just two people forced into something neither of them wanted by two old men. Well, it's time to stop the charade."

She winced. He felt his throat constrict but, damn it, somebody had to say it.

She looked away. A long moment passed. Then she turned her face to his. Her expression startled him. She was calm. Composed. She looked…she looked relieved.

"Thank you for speaking the truth." There was no tremor in her voice now. No tears in those violet eyes. "And you are right. There is no sense in continuing this…this charade. I would be grateful if you phoned your attorney tomorrow."

He nodded. She went up the stairs. He watched until she vanished from sight, heard her door open, heard it close…

And knew he had just lost the only thing in the world that mattered.

"Chiara," he said, and then he shouted her name and ran for the stairs, taking them two at a time, racing down the hall, throwing open the door to her bedroom. "Sweetheart. Chiara, I didn't mean it. I didn't—"

She turned toward him. She was sobbing; her face was wet with tears.

"Baby," he whispered, and then she was in his arms.

CHAPTER ELEVEN

RAFE gathered his wife tightly in his arms, his heart soaring as she looped her arms around his neck and pressed her body to his.

He knew that his anger had been nothing but a pathetic attempt at hiding the truth. He wanted her, had wanted her from that first kiss in Sicily. And she wanted him.

He was not going to turn away from that tonight. The bed was only a few steps away.

He could take her to it, strip her naked, tear off his own clothes and bury himself in her. One deep thrust and she would be his.

Some still-functioning part of his brain told him he owed her much, much more.

She was innocent. A virgin. And she'd been told things about what happened between men and women that had terrified her.

He had to make what came next perfect. As perfect as her innocence.

"Chiara," he said softly.

Slowly she opened her eyes. The pupils were enormous, deep and dark and filled with all the questions a man could ever want to be asked. With all his heart, Rafe hoped he had answers that would please her.

"Chiara," he said again, and kissed her. Once. Twice, his lips brushing gently over hers, each time lingering just a little longer until she gave a sigh of pleasure and her lips parted.

"That's the way," he murmured. "Yes, sweet-heart. Open for me. Taste me. Let me taste you."

He could feel her hesitation. Then, slowly, she let him in.

The need to tumble her onto the bed swept through him with such power that he felt his muscles constrict. His big, powerful body shuddered.

"Raffaele?"

"It's all right. I just— I want—" He framed her face between his hands, lifted it to him and kissed her, his mouth hot and open over hers, his tongue seeking the sweetness that awaited him.

Her taste filled him. Honey. Cream. Vanilla. And, mingled with it, the taste of a woman aroused.

He whispered her name. She moved closer.

Her hands crept up his chest to his shoulders, and he lifted her into him. He felt the delicate weight of her breasts against the hard wall of his chest, felt the feminine convexity of her belly pressed against the taut flatness of his.

Felt his erection rise and swell until he groaned with the almost unbearable pleasure of it.

Chiara gasped. Clutched his shoulders. Said his name again, and he could hear shock, wonder, apprehension in the single whispered word.

He was like stone. And all of this was new to his wife.

He took his lips from hers. Held her by the shoulders. She whimpered, tried to move closer, and though it killed him to stop her, he did.

"Why—" Her voice was low and thready. "Why did you stop kissing me? Did I do it wrong? If I did—"

"No," he said quickly. "God, no! There's no right way or wrong way to kiss." Another deep breath. "But I don't want to hurry you, sweetheart, or frighten you."

"I am not afraid of you," she whispered. "It is the rest. The…the touching."

"We can stop now," he said, and wondered if

a man who was a liar could still be a candidate for sainthood.

Her response was too soft to hear.

She looked up into his eyes. "I don't want to stop. I want to know what it is men and women do together."

"Not men and women," he said gruffly. "Us. You and me."

Her smile filled his heart. "*Sì*. You and me, Raffaele. Show me, please."

He brought her hand to his lips, pressed kisses to her fingertips, then brought her hand between them and laid it lightly over his erection. Her breath hissed between her teeth; her palm cupped the hard bulge in his jeans.

Rafe shuddered and Chiara snatched back her hand. "Did I hurt you?"

"No," he said gruffly, clasping her hand, putting it on him again. "No, you didn't hurt me. I—" he swallowed hard "—I love what you just did. Touching me that way… Do you know what it means, that I'm hard like that?"

He watched her teeth worry her bottom lip. He longed to do that for her. Bite gently into that delicate flesh.

"It means—" Her voice was so low he had to

bend to her to hear it. "It means you…you want to do things to me."

Rafe swallowed an oath. "It means that I want to do things *with* you. To touch each other in ways that bring us both pleasure."

She nodded, dipped her head so that her curls became a curtain that hid her from him.

"Do it, then," she whispered.

Rafe took a long breath, expelled it slowly enough to give him time to think. Then he put his hand under Chiara's chin and lifted her face to his.

"Hey," he said gently, "this isn't a visit to the dentist." That bought him a smile, as he'd hoped it would. "Chiara. Sweetheart, we're not going to do anything you don't want to do."

"That's just it. I do not know what I want or do not want." She lifted her hands to his chest. Could she feel the race of his heart? "I only know that…that something happens when you kiss me, Raffaele. I feel…I feel—"

"Tell me."

Her face colored. "I feel things. Sensations. In…in parts of me…" A laugh that was close to a sob caught in her throat. "I cannot talk about it. Talking about my body is—"

She gasped as he cupped her breast, gave a

little cry, almost pulled back, but he slid an arm around her, held her while his fingers moved gently, unerringly over her nipple. He could feel it budding even through the harsh, unyielding cotton of her dress. She moaned. Her lashes drooped, became inky-black crescents against her cheeks.

"Do you feel something when I do this?" he said hoarsely.

She looked up at him, her face striped with color. "Yes. Oh *Dio*, yes. Like that. Just like—"

"Where do you feel it?"

"There. Where you are touching me. And… and elsewhere. Lower than my breasts, Raffaele. I feel it—"

She cried out as he ran his hand down her body, to the juncture of her thighs. He had touched her there before but all of that had gone too quickly. None of what would happen now would be quick. He would bring her slowly, slowly to pleasure, and never mind his own desires.

This first time, only her needs, her pleasure, her fulfillment mattered.

"Here?" he said thickly. "What do you feel, baby?"

"I feel—I feel—heat. A tingle. It is what

happens during a storm, when you stand outside and the lightning strikes on the hills and you can almost feel the electricity in your bones. Do you know what I mean, Raffaele?"

He knew. It was how he felt now, as if a storm of incredible magnitude were building inside him, the tension almost more than he could tolerate.

He answered the whispered question by urging her thighs apart, just enough so he could cup her over the stiff fabric of her dress. She gasped, her eyes wild. "I feel as if…as if I am melting. There. Where your hand is."

He could feel his muscles trembling. Her innocence was enough to send him to the edge of control, but he would not let that happen.

"Your body is readying itself for me, sweetheart. For us."

He moved his hand and she gasped again, then buried her face against his shoulder. "I never knew—"

"No," Rafe said with a little laugh, "neither did I." It was true. He'd been with a lot of women and enjoyed them all, but this, what was happening now, what he was feeling now…

"I think I am burning up," she whispered.

So was he. When she returned tomorrow

morning, Mrs. O'Hara might well find this bedroom in ashes.

"I think—" He cleared his throat. "Why don't we get some of this clothing out of the way?"

"Is it time for me to…to undress?"

"Leave that to me," he said huskily.

Did everything she owned have a thousand buttons? Did the buttons always have to be so small, especially when his fingers were so big and clumsy? It took forever to undo the first button. The second. The third…

The dress began falling open, revealing her to him, and he forgot about buttons, buttonholes, the size of his fingers. He skimmed the back of his hand down her throat, then followed the same path with light kisses. Her pulse, in the tender hollow where her neck met her collarbones, danced beneath his mouth and he exulted at the feel of it.

At last the buttons were all undone. Rafe freed her of the dress and let it fall to her feet.

Her bra, her panties were white cotton, just as they'd been that first time. Except he hadn't undressed her then, he'd torn the dress from her body.

All the more reason to do this with the greatest care. He would touch her as if she were made of the most delicate crystal.

He would. He would—but the curve of her breasts above that modest bra was lush. And, God, he could see the dark outline of her nipples…

Rafe bent his head and closed his mouth around the tip of one cotton-covered breast. Chiara's cry of pleasure almost tore him apart.

On a low growl, he scooped her into his arms, carried her to the bed and laid her down. He kicked off his mocs, yanked his sweater over his head and tossed it aside. Chiara's gaze flew over him, as hot and urgent as a caress. He came down on the bed beside her and kissed her, his mouth drinking the honey from hers, his hands learning her body.

Her bra closed in the front, and he sent up a silent thank-you to whatever god had sent him that gift. She didn't try to stop him as he undid the clasp but when the bra came away, her hands fluttered up to cover her breasts.

He shook his head, gently caught her wrists and brought her hands to her sides.

"Let me see you," he whispered. "I need to see you, Chiara."

She lay back. She was breathing hard. He could feel her eyes on him as he looked at her.

Ah, she was beautiful. More beautiful than he had imagined. Her breasts were round, with dusty pink crests already peaking as they begged for the heat of his mouth.

He brought his gaze to her face, watched her eyes as he cupped one breast, groaning as he felt the perfect weight of it in his hand. Her pupils widened, then seemed to swallow her irises as he moved his thumb over the tip.

"Raffaele…"

Her voice was shaky. He stroked her nipple again, then captured it between his thumb and index finger, gently caressed it.

Chiara moaned.

"Do you like that?" he said thickly.

A sob broke in her throat. She moaned again as he increased the pressure of his caress, lowered his head, closed his lips around the straining nipple and drew it deep into the heat of his mouth.

She said something in Italian. He didn't understand the words, but the arching of her body, the feel of her hand clasping the nape of his neck as he sucked on her beaded flesh, told him all he needed to know.

He drew back. She made a sweet sound of protest.

"Don't leave me," she whispered.

"No," he said fiercely. "Never."

It took only seconds to unzip his jeans, get rid of them and his shorts. He saw her eyes flash to his genitals, then widen and fly to his face.

He'd never considered what a woman might feel the first time she saw a fully aroused male. Now he did. Could it be frightening? Maybe, especially if the woman was completely innocent. And if the guy was big.

He was.

He'd always taken a kind of arrogant male pride in his size. Now he realized that what might make an experienced woman smile with anticipation could make his Chiara feel terror.

He took her hand. Brought it to his lips, pressed a kiss into the palm. "Don't be afraid," he said softly. "This is just another part of me." He kissed her hand again, then slowly brought it to his erection. She hesitated and then he felt the first, cool brush of her fingers.

It took all the determination he possessed not to throw back his head and groan.

"See?" he said, fighting to keep his voice steady. Slowly her hand closed around his turgid length. Rafe bit his lip.

"You are so hard here," she said in wonder. "And yet, so soft."

"Not soft," he said, trying for a little levity. "Not—"

Ah. She moved her hand. Up. Down. Up...

He caught her wrist. "Don't," he said gruffly. "Or this will end too quickly." He pressed a light kiss to her mouth. "Besides," he whispered, "this isn't fair."

"It isn't?"

He smiled. "I'm naked. You're not."

He kissed her again, deeper, longer, and as he did, he slid her panties off. Then he traced the path they'd taken with his hand. The lovely indentation of her waist. The curve of her hip.

The delicate curls that guarded her feminine heart.

Her fingers clamped on his.

"I won't hurt you, Chiara," he said softly.

Slowly she took her hand away.

Rafe stroked those curls. Soothed her with soft words. Softer kisses. She was silken under his touch, warm and, yes, wet. Wet for him.

He drew back and looked at her. His throat constricted.

Naked, she was everything he had imagined. She was an El Greco painting come to life, Praxiteles's Aphrodite made all the more exquisite because she was flesh and blood, not cold marble.

"Chiara," he whispered, and he moved down her body and pressed his lips to that sweet, female delta.

Her hands flew to his shoulders. "No! You must not—"

He caught her wrists and went on kissing her. Gradually, her hands relaxed in his grasp. Her breathing quickened. And when he gently parted her delicate folds, she sobbed his name.

"It is too much," she said brokenly. "Too much…"

He knew it wasn't nearly enough. He wanted to see her fly into the sky, then fly into it again…with him.

"Open your legs for me," he said in a voice so rough it didn't seem his own.

"I can't," she said breathlessly. "People do not—"

"Open your legs, baby. For me."

Slowly she did as he'd asked. He touched her with reverence, parted her again, groaned when he saw the tender bud of her clitoris.

"Chiara," he said softly, and he put his mouth against her.

Wild little cries burst from her throat. She began to weep. He froze but then he felt her hands in his hair, holding him to her instead of pushing him away. As if he would ever take his mouth from her, he thought in wonder. From her taste. Her scent. She was everything a man could ever want or dream.

She was his.

He slipped his hands under her, lifted her higher into the passionate intimacy of his kiss. He felt her shudder and then she screamed his name and he knew she had glimpsed the burning rays of the sun.

Now, he thought, and he moved over her, positioned himself between her thighs and entered her, teeth gritted with the determination to do it slowly.

He didn't want to hurt her, didn't want to hurt her—

Her legs closed around his hips, urging him on.

Rafe flung his head back, thrust deep, flew over the edge of the earth and took his wife with him.

Chiara lay beneath Raffaele's hard body, her arms still holding him to her.

His heartbeat was slowing or maybe it was

hers. They were so close that she couldn't tell the difference. And he was still inside her.

She closed her eyes.

A man, inside her. No. It was *this* man who was inside her. This man, who had taken her on a journey so intense she'd never wanted it to end.

This man.

Her husband.

The thought sent a sweet tremor through her. Raffaele stirred. Without thinking, she tightened her arms around him.

"Hey," he said softly, and she blushed as she realized he wanted to get off her. Of course he did. Her mother had told her some things that were obviously incorrect but some were surely accurate.

For instance, when a man finished with a woman, he had no further wish to remain in her bed. This was Raffaele's bed, not hers, but the principle was the same.

What an idiot I am, she thought, and let him go.

He rolled off her, but he didn't go anywhere. Instead he gathered her into his arms and drew her close. Surprised, she let him do it—she loved having him do it—but she wasn't foolish enough to think he'd hold her for very long.

"Are you okay?"

She nodded and burrowed a little closer, her nose just at the juncture of his shoulder and arm. She loved the smell of him there. Back home, there'd been times the very scent of a man's body made her belly knot and her throat clench but this was different. Rafe's scent was masculine and musky and exciting.

"Chiara?" He ran one hand into her hair as he cupped her cheek. "Did I hurt you?"

He had, at that last amazing moment, but she'd have died rather than have stopped him. The feel of him, deep inside her… It had been pleasure so incredible that even remembering it made her tremble.

"Damn," he said gruffly, "I did."

"No. It's all right. I did not mind."

"You didn't mind?" Suddenly she was no longer lying cradled against him, she was on her back and he was leaning over her. "Damn it, you have every right to mind," he said gruffly. "I tried to go slow but—"

"Raffaele." She smiled. "It was wonderful."

He grinned. Such a becoming grin! But then, why wouldn't it be? He was beautiful.

"Yeah?"

"Wonderful," she said softly.

"The next time we make love, it'll be even more wonderful."

Her heart filled. They had not had sex, they had made love. How wrong her mother had been!

"What?" he said, smiling at her.

She smiled back. "Nothing. I was just thinking…"

"Me, too." His smile tilted. "About next time."

"I am glad you are thinking that, Raffaele," she whispered. "Very glad."

Rafe kissed her. She sighed and opened her mouth to his. His kiss deepened, his hand cupped her breast and her nipple engorged at his touch.

"Oh," she said softly, "oh, yes…"

He slid his hand down her body. Cupped her. Slipped a finger inside those plump folds… And saw her wince. Cursing softly, he gathered her into his arms.

"See? I did hurt you. Forgive me, baby. It's much too soon."

"No." Her cheeks turned pink. "If you would like to…to make love again—"

"I would like to make love straight into tomorrow," he said solemnly. "But this is your first time and you need to take it easy."

She would have protested but he kissed her

again, then rose from the bed. She sat up, the sheet drawn over her breasts, and watched him. Had he changed his mind? Was he leaving her now?

No. He was not. Unashamedly naked, he went into the connecting bathroom and shut the door. Chiara lay back against the pillows. She felt boneless and happy and exhausted. It was as if she had experienced a miracle. That sex—that making love could be like this…

But it was not really love. Love was not what Raffaele—what her husband felt for her, and that was all right because…because it was not what she felt for him, either.

Tears welled in her eyes. And what for? What reason was there to weep? Something that had begun as a disaster had turned into something, yes, wonderful. She was free of her father, of San Giuseppe. And she was with a man who had taught her that sex could be the most wonderful experience of a woman's life—

Even if he was not going to be in her life…

"Hey."

Raffaele's voice was soft. He was standing beside the bed, holding a small basin and a towel.

"Sweetheart. Why are you crying?"

226 RAFFAELE: TAMING HIS TEMPESTUOUS VIRGIN

"I am not crying. I am just— I am weepy. Did no one ever tell you that women get weepy when they are happy?" She sniffed back her tears and hurried to change the subject. "Thank you for the basin of water but—"

"But you're going to take care of things yourself."

"*Sì*. As I should. As I— Raffaele, that is not for you to do."

But he was already sitting beside her, the wash-cloth in his hand.

"Yes," he said softly, "it is for me to do." He brought the warm, wet cloth to her thighs, nudged them gently apart and began laving her with it. "I took your virginity."

She smiled a little. "Yes," she whispered. "You did."

Rafe rinsed the cloth in the basin, wrung it out again and carefully used it on her once more. There were tiny drops of blood on her thighs and on the cloth. The sight of her blood, the knowledge that his lovemaking had been the reason she had shed it, was almost overwhelming.

He put the cloth aside, gently dried her with the soft towel, got into the bed and gathered her in his arms.

"Shut your eyes, sweetheart. You've had a long couple of days."

"Mmm."

"Just…just let me kiss you first…"

His lips closed over hers. She sighed with pleasure. His mouth moved lower. Along her throat. She sighed again. His mouth found her breasts and her sighs became moans.

"Raffaele," she said, as he drew a nipple deep into his mouth. "Raffaele…"

"It's too soon," he said thickly, but she slipped a hand between them, touched him, caressed him, and he groaned and moved over her. "Are you sure?"

Her answer came not in words but in the stroke of her fingers, the arch of her spine, the mingling of her breath with his.

He drew away, took something from the night-stand drawer. Chiara knew what it was.

A condom.

He had not used one the first time. It was her safe time of month—Miss Ellis had taught her the basics of biology—but she thought she would not have cared if he had made her pregnant. This was her Raffaele.

Her husband.

She watched as he tore open the little pack and rolled the condom on. She wanted to do it for him. To touch him. To explore his hard flesh with her hands, her mouth…

She reached for him as he came back to her, and he entered her slowly, eased into her with such care that his muscles trembled until, at last, he was deep, deep inside her.

Could a woman die of pleasure? If she did, it would be worth what she felt now.

The rhythm he set was hard and urgent but she stayed with him, thrust for thrust. She cried out, arched from the bed and, seconds later, cried out again as her Raffaele took her with him into that place where the sun blazed forever.

"Chiara," he whispered. "My beautiful, beautiful bride."

Tears again rose in her eyes. She blinked them back and returned his tender kisses as he drew her close in his arms. Moments later his breathing was deep and even, but she lay awake for a very long time, torn between incredible joy and heartbreaking despair.

Raffaele was her husband.

Except, he was not. Not really.

And this, all of this, could not last.

CHAPTER TWELVE

Was there a specific protocol for a woman's behavior when she woke in a man's arms?

Did you lie motionless until he was awake? Slip free of his embrace, gather up your clothes and tiptoe from the room? What if all that shifting around woke him?

What did people say to each other after they'd spent the night making love?

They'd made love again and again, Chiara thought with a little shudder of pleasure. And each time had been different and even better than the last.

How could her mother have been so wrong? This was not pain or submission or humiliation. This was pure joy, a heart-stopping, breathless climb to the very top of a mountain and then a long, dizzying flight to the stars.

At least, it was when Raffaele Orsini was your lover.

During the night she'd awakened to his kisses. She'd shot from sleep with her heart pounding, struggling against the alien, male touch.

"No," she'd said sharply, and he'd framed her face with his hands.

"Chiara. Sweetheart, it's me."

Slowly she'd became aware of the familiarity of the hard body poised just over hers. His scent. His features. His skin, smooth and warm over taut muscle.

"Raffaele," she'd whispered.

"I'm sorry, Chiara. I didn't mean to frighten you."

"No. You didn't. I just… What time is it?"

"It's late. Very late. You should be asleep."

She'd smiled, lifted her hand, stroked it against the sexy stubble on his jaw. "Mmm. So should you."

"Soon," he'd whispered, between kisses. "But first, a kiss…"

One kiss. Then another. She'd lifted her arms and wound them around his neck. His kisses deepened. Her response intensified. That part of him she had so feared was already hard against her belly. Now it swelled even more.

Why had she ever been afraid of this? Being held so intimately. Being kissed as if you were a man's only hope of salvation. The stroke of a strong, callused hand.

The pulsing, aroused flesh that was so beautifully, fiercely male.

"Raffaele," she'd whispered.

Shamelessly she'd wrapped one leg high around his. He'd said her name in a voice so filled with desire that it had been like a caress, slipped a hand beneath her and raised her into him. When his erect penis had nudged against her, she'd caught her breath.

Instantly he pulled back. "Forgive me, sweetheart. You're sore."

"I ache," she'd whispered, "but not because I am sore, Raffaele, I ache for you. I want you inside me." Overcome with embarrassment, she'd buried her face against his shoulder. "Oh. I should not have said—"

"Yes," he'd said fiercely, cupping the back of her head, lifting her face to his until their eyes met. "You should. I love hearing you say that you want me."

"I do," she'd replied, "I want you, want you, want—"

Their mouths fused. Moments later he had been deep inside her.

Remembering, Chiara smiled. Actually, she

was a little tender, but it was a wonderful tenderness, a reminder of her husband's lovemaking…

Her smile faded.

Her husband. Her very temporary husband. How had she forgotten that? More to the point, how had she forgotten that, despite his gentleness, his kindness, her husband was in the same "profession" as her father?

She wanted to weep. Her mother had things wrong. Sex was not ugly. It was a drug to make a woman forget the truth.

Quickly she pushed the blankets aside and moved out of Raffaele's embrace. There was enough early-morning light in the room so she could see her clothes, discarded on the floor. If she was quiet…

"Hey."

She froze, her dress clasped against her body, her back to the bed.

"What time is it?" Raffaele yawned; the bedding rustled. She knew he must be reaching for the clock on the nightstand. "Chiara," he groaned, "it's barely six-thirty." His voice dropped to a husky purr. "Come back to bed."

She took a steadying breath, forced the mental

image of her husband's muscled, beautiful body from her mind. The important thing was to speak calmly. She had behaved foolishly, but it would not happen again. He needed to understand that.

"Six-thirty is late for me. At home, I would already be in the kitchen, making coffee."

His chuckle was low and sexy. "We tried that, remember? I'm the one who makes the coffee around here."

"It does not matter who makes the coffee. What matters is that your housekeeper will be arriving soon."

"And?"

"And I do not wish her to find us like this."

More rustling. Was he getting out of bed? *Please, no. Let him stay where he is. At least, let him put on some clothes.*

"Not a problem, sweetheart. Mrs. O'Hara doesn't come in today. Even if she did, she never comes into my bedroom. Well, into a bedroom with a closed door."

"Certainly not. I am sure she is under strict orders not to disturb you and whatever woman you have brought home for the—"

"Is that what's troubling you?"

"No. It is not. Why would it trouble me?" Why, indeed? Why had she even said such a foolish—

He came up behind her, dropped his hands lightly on her shoulders. "Are you trying to count all the women who've spent the night with me?"

"No," she said again. "I already told you that."

Slowly he turned her toward him. Her heartbeat quickened. Yes, he was naked. Beautifully naked, his shoulders and arms taut with muscle, a whorl of dark hair over his hard-planed chest, a flat abdomen leading down to his sex.

"I'm not going to lie to you," he said quietly. "There've been women here."

Why did the admission hurt? "Really, Raffaele, you owe me no explanation."

"Maybe not. But it's important to me that you understand. I've never spent a night like this one, sweetheart. And I've never awakened wishing the night had not yet ended."

She didn't answer. She wouldn't even meet his eyes. Something was wrong, but Rafe had no idea what that something was.

"Chiara."

He put his hand under his wife's chin and lifted her face to his. Yes. She was troubled. So was he.

Something had changed inside him, during the long night. It had to do with their making love but there was more to it than that. He wished to hell he knew what it was, but whatever had changed, whatever he felt, was just out of reach.

He only knew that he was happy.

Incredibly happy.

He said Chiara's name again, bent his head and kissed her. At first she didn't respond. Then she sighed and kissed him back.

He smiled. "Good morning, sweetheart," he said softly.

Her smile was tremulous. "Good morning, Raffaele."

His eyes moved over her face. As always, it was bare of makeup and it hit him that he couldn't recall seeing a woman without makeup, even after a long night in bed. Falco joked about it. The 5:00 a.m. face, he called it, because it was always freshly painted on by the time a man opened his eyes. Women were programmed, Falco said, to wake at dawn so they'd have time to scrub off last night's war paint and put on today's.

Chiara had put nothing on her face. She hadn't fixed her hair, either, as women always did. It went with the 5:00 a.m. face—the perfect straight fall or the artfully tumbled curls.

Not his wife. Her hair was a dark nimbus of silk.

Rafe's gut clenched. It was tough to decide what he wanted most right now. To carry her back to bed and make love to her, or simply to hold her close in his arms.

And there it was again, that sad expression in her lovely eyes. Did she regret their long, wonderful night?

"Sweetheart?" He hesitated. "Are you sorry we made love?"

He'd expected a quick answer, a smile and a no, and maybe a touch of her lips against his. But the seconds slipped past, and just when he thought he was going to go crazy, she shook her head and melted against him.

"The thing is," she said, in a small voice, "the thing is, I do not understand any of this."

His sense of relief was enormous. He pulled back, just far enough so he could see her face, and flashed a wicked, sexy grin.

"Which part don't you understand, baby? I'll be happy to help."

"I am serious, Raffaele. I mean, we hardly

know each other. Our marriage is not..." She couldn't say it, and wasn't that silly? "Our marriage is not a normal one. We are only together because you were my Sir Galahad."

"Sorry to disappoint you, but I doubt if Galahad's armor was as tarnished as mine."

"And that is another thing." Her voice was low. "Your...your occupation."

His eyebrows rose. "Well, I'll admit, lots of people don't think much of guys in my business right now, but—"

"You have been so good to me. So gentle." Her eyes searched his. "So how could you be one of them?"

"One of who?"

"You know. You are part of...of— What is it called here? My father's organization. Your father's. How could you be you and be part of that, as well?"

It took a couple of seconds before he figured it out. She still thought he was a hoodlum. He would have laughed, but he sensed that this wasn't really funny.

"Okay," he said briskly, "here's what we're gonna do. Shower. Get dressed. Then we'll go out for breakfast and after that, I'll show you what it is I do for a living. What I *really* do for a living, sweetheart, as opposed to what you think I do."

"I know what you do, Raffaele. Didn't I just tell you that?"

"Yes. You did." He kissed her. Just for good measure, he kissed her again. "And," he said softly, "I can see that it really matters to you."

"Of course it matters," she said with indignation. "I— You and I—we did things…"

"Amazing things," he said huskily. "Incredible things." He gave her a slow, tender kiss. "And we'll do them again, sweetheart, but first I'm going to show you who I really am."

"I keep telling you—"

He silenced her with another kiss. "I know you do," he said gently. "And now, I'm telling you, baby. Give me the benefit of the doubt, okay?"

Chiara nodded. "Okay," she murmured, because maybe she was wrong about him. She *had* to be wrong. How could she, of all people, have made love with a man who was as evil as her father? How could she have lain in his arms?

Most of all, she thought, most of all…

Most of all, how could she be falling in love with him?

* * *

Rafe wanted her to shower with him.

She refused.

He knew it would take him less than a minute to change her mind. His wife was the most responsive woman he'd ever been with. All he had to do was touch her, kiss her. But if they ended up back in bed, he'd feel even guiltier about how many times he'd made love to her during the night.

So he made do with a kiss. Well, a few kisses. Her eyelids. Her cheeks. Her delectable mouth and, finally, her breasts. She put up a little struggle, a couple of *You must not, Raffaele* whispers, but she moaned when he tugged away that ratty dress she clutched like a shield and touched his lips to first one delicate nipple and then the other.

Stopping was sheer hell, but knowing she didn't want him to stop was a gift that made it worthwhile.

"Later," he said softly, and then he spun her toward the door and told her to hurry up and get ready to go out.

She bristled.

"I do not take orders, Raff— Oh!"

It was the reaction he'd hoped for, the indignant "Oh" when he swatted her lightly on her naked butt—she was clutching her dress again and she seemed to have forgotten it only covered her front—and then a shocked gasp when he followed it up with a quick kiss on that same place.

She all but ran for the bathroom. He chuckled. He knew he'd pay for it later.

At least, he hoped he would.

Twenty minutes later he was showered and dressed.

Jeans. A dark blue sweater and a leather jacket, because the day looked bright but he could see the tops of the trees in the park swaying under the wind. He scooped up his keys and wallet, then headed downstairs. Chiara wouldn't be ready, of course. He knew women. She would need another twenty, thirty minutes. He'd wait for her near the elevator. It was safer than waiting for her upstairs where all he had to do was go down the hall, turn the doorknob to her room…

But his wife was waiting for *him*. She'd tamed her hair, damn it, pulling it back into another of those knots, and she was wearing one of those black dresses.

Something must have shown in his face. She

blushed a little, brushed her hand down the length of the dress.

"I know this is not what New York women wear, but—"

Rafe wrapped his arm around her shoulders and kissed her. It was the kind of opening he'd been waiting for, and he wasn't about to let it go by.

"Breakfast can wait," he said. "First we'll deal with what New York women wear."

It was still early. Too early for Saks to be open but why would that stop him? He had a client who knew a guy who a guy…

By the time they'd reached the lobby, he'd made a couple of calls on his cell. And by the time they reached Saks, a polite gentleman in an expensive suit was waiting at a side door to let them in.

Chiara balked. "What are we doing here, Raffaele?"

"I told you," he said easily, "we're going to see what it is New York women wear."

She dug in her heels. "This must be an expensive store."

He shrugged. "Maybe."

Her jaw firmed. "I cannot afford it. I have not had time to find a buyer for my mother's jewels."

Did she actually think he'd let her sell those

jewels? She was his wife. For now, anyway. And a husband supplied his wife's clothes.

"You can argue with me later," he said, and he took her hand and led her inside the store.

Her soft ooh's and aaah's made him smile as the man in the suit led them through displays of silk scarves and accessories, past endless counters of perfume and cosmetics until they reached the elevators. One was waiting, and the three of them stepped inside.

"Where do we get off?" his wife whispered.

A good question. He hadn't asked; he'd simply told the guy his client had put him in touch with that he wanted to buy a few things for a lady...

The doors opened. An acre of garments stretched ahead but—Rafe breathed a sigh of relief—a guide was waiting.

Well, a salesclerk. A saleswoman. An associate. Whatever you called an angel who greeted you with a smile and gave no sign that her newest customer looked like she'd stepped off the ancient streets of Sicily.

"Good morning," she said pleasantly. "My name is Nella. How may I help you?"

Rafe made his first mistake. He asked Chiara what she needed.

Her chin came up. "Nothing!"

He nodded. "And maybe that's just as well," he said, eyes wide with innocence. "I mean, even if you did need, oh, I don't know…let's say, some sweaters. Jeans. A jacket. A couple of dresses…"

"I just said, Raffaele, I do not need—"

"Right. And I said that was good because I don't think they carry your size here."

"Raffaele. Perhaps you did not—" Her brow furrowed. "Excuse me?"

"You don't, do you, Nella?" He looked at the saleswoman. "You don't have anything, well, um, anything in a size big enough for my wife?"

Nella's lips twitched. "Well, Mr. Orsini, I must admit, I'd have to check."

Chiara was bristling.

"I am a small size," she said coldly. "A very small size. I am not a stick, which is perhaps the way you prefer your women, Signor Orsini, but I can assure you—"

"What you are," Rafe said, pulling her into his arms, "is gorgeous." He kissed her. And kissed her. Nella bit back a smile and drifted toward a display of cashmere sweaters. When he finally ended the kiss, what he wanted more than his next breath was to tell Nella to go away, but he behaved himself, pointed his wife toward the saleswoman and stepped safely out of the line of fire.

It was a new experience, sitting on a sofa too small and dainty for a man his size, quietly asking himself what in hell he was doing.

He had bought things for women before. Necklaces. Bracelets. Flowers and perfume and chocolate. Okay, correction. He'd had his PA buy them. He had never been part of the selection process.

A new experience, absolutely.

He felt weird at first, sitting there like some kind of potentate, nodding each time Chiara appeared. *Appeared* was too generous a word. Nella sort of prodded her out of the dressing room. At the start, anyway.

After a while, though, as the parade of cashmere sweaters and jeans, wool trousers and silk blouses, long dresses and short dresses kept going, there seemed to be less prodding and more, well, more prancing.

She might never admit it, but his wife was enjoying this game of dress up.

So was he.

She looked spectacular in everything and when

Nella began adding shoes and boots with heels high enough to make him salivate, he wondered why nobody had ever come up with an evening's entertainment called *Watching a Beautiful Woman Parade before Her Lover.*

Parade before her husband.

Well, he wasn't. Not really. He wasn't anybody's husband. He wouldn't be, not for a very long time, certainly not at the behest of his old man.

"…the last one, Raffaele."

Rafe blinked. His wife stood before him. Her hair had come loose of that abominable knot. It spilled over her shoulders like long waves of dark silk. She wore a cashmere sweater the color of garnets, tight jeans and black leather boots that could only look better than they already did if she'd worn them without the sweater and the jeans and, damn it, he was on the verge of embarrassing himself.

"What?" he said, and cleared his throat.

"I said, this is the last outfit. You must decide which one we should buy."

He knew there was only one correct answer. He also knew better than to offer it in front of her. Instead, he rose to his feet.

"This looks nice," he said, as casually as possible.

She beamed. "I think so, too."

He nodded and turned to Nella. "My wife will take these things. In fact, she'll wear them now. Just add a jacket. Leather, to match the boots."

Nella nodded and hurried off. Chiara leveled a look at him.

"Raffaele," she said, the single word filled with warning.

"What?" he said innocently. "New York's cool this time of year."

"I have a coat."

Nella hurried back with a leather jacket. "Just try this on," he said. "Please."

Knowledge of the night they'd shared was in his eyes. Chiara's expression softened. "I will try it on, but I am not promising anything."

She slipped into the jacket and turned to the mirror. Rafe watched her reflection in the glass, saw her lips form a perfect O, heard her little sigh of pleasure. It struck him that there had not been much pleasure in his wife's life. The realization made him want to return to Sicily and shake her father until his teeth rattled.

The saleswoman raised her eyebrows. "Don't you like the jacket, sir?"

Rafe took a steadying breath. "I like it a lot."

Forcing a smile, he took his Amex Black card from his wallet and handed it to her. "We'll take everything," he said quietly.

Nella's eyebrows rose another inch. *"Everything?"*

"Everything," he said, putting his finger to his lips. "Have it all delivered to my home. Understand?"

The woman's smile was wide and gentle. "I most certainly do, Mr. Orsini."

Good. Excellent. At least someone understood, because he damned well didn't. He had a wife who wasn't really his wife. A wife he didn't want. A wife forced upon him by the machinations of her father and his.

And yet, just looking at her filled him with joy. With delight. With...with—

He frowned and barked Chiara's name. She spun toward him.

He knew what he had to tell her. That it was getting late. That they had things to do. That he had no idea why he'd said he'd show her how he actually earned his living because what he was going to do was phone Marilyn Sayers's office and demand an immediate appointment so they could get moving with this divorce thing.

"Raffaele? Did you want to tell me something?"

"Yes," he said gruffly. 'I wanted to tell you…to tell you—" A muscle knotted in his jaw. "I wanted to tell you that you look beautiful."

Chiara smiled. "It is the jacket. And the sweater. And—"

"The hell it is," he said, and then she was in his arms and he was kissing her with a hunger that exceeded anything he'd ever imagined.

CHAPTER THIRTEEN

HE MADE a call on his cell phone while Chiara stepped into the cab he'd hailed, told the doorman to expect a delivery from Saks, that the porter was to take everything to his penthouse and stack it all in the master bedroom.

Then he climbed into the cab, took his wife's hand and told the cabby to take them to Balthazar, a Soho bistro where the morning meal was as much a ritual as an art.

He was greeted warmly by name and led to his usual table. It offered a modicum of privacy, though privacy was in short supply here, but the crowds, the noise, were part of the charm.

The busboy brought their menus. Chiara said thank you, opened hers but didn't look at it. She was too busy looking around the busy room.

Rafe didn't look at his menu, either. He was too busy looking at his wife.

Lord, how beautiful she was! And it wasn't the new clothes; it was her. She was beautiful and filled with life. She'd chattered away almost nonstop once they left Saks, excited by the sights, the architecture, the crowds.

"Such a city," she'd said with delight. "So filled with people! Where can they all be going in such a hurry?"

Where am *I* going? Rafe had thought.

Not just out to breakfast. He was heading somewhere at the speed of light, a place he had never been before, and if that made no sense, he was stuck with it. The only sure thing was that he was heading there because of his wife.

He knew it was foolish to think of her that way, but legally that was who she was. His wife. Mrs. Rafe Orsini. Mrs. *Raffaele* Orsini, and when had he come to prefer the sound of his actual given name? He'd never felt comfortable with it, maybe because it had always been a reminder of his ancestry and all he'd imagined went with it.

The way his wife said it, "Raffaele" was a benediction. His wife. His beautiful, bright, exciting wife…

"Oh, Raffaele, this is a wonderful place!"

Chiara was leaning toward him, smiling. He reached for her hand and brought it to his lips.

"I'm glad you like it."

"Do you come here often? It seems a long way from where you live."

The waiter hovered beside them. Rafe waved him off.

"It is, but my office is just a couple of blocks from here."

Her smile dimmed. "Your office."

"Yes. So I've gotten into the habit of stopping here for breakfast when I have the chance."

"You don't work from home like…like—"

"Like your old man or mine? No. My operation's too big for that, though there are times I wish I could."

"Oh."

Her "oh" sounded flat. He knew what she was thinking, that his "operation" must be even more powerful than her father's. Let her think it. It would only increase her surprise and, he hoped, her pleasure when she saw the Orsini Brothers building and his handsome office.

"So," he said briskly, "what would you like for breakfast?"

Chiara looked down at her menu. She could

feel the joy in her heart draining away. All this—
the night in her husband's arms, the shopping trip
this morning…

A dream.

She must not forget that again.

No matter what Raffaele made her feel, he was
part of a world she hated. He had come to San
Giuseppe to do his father's bidding because he was
a good soldier in the Sicilian sense of the word.

It was just as well this so-called marriage would
end as soon as his attorney returned to the city.

Suddenly the thought of eating made her feel
sick. Carefully she put down the menu.

"Actually, Raffaele, I am not very—I am not
terribly hungry."

She tried to pull her hand free of his. He
wouldn't let her. Instead he leaned close.

"Chiara," he said softly, "the day's just begun.
Don't sit in judgment on me yet." He kissed her
palm. "Okay?"

Their eyes met. Her husband looked handsome
and earnest and…and, God oh God, she was not
falling in love with him, she was already in love
with him. Desperately in love with him, and
suddenly she knew that it didn't matter if he was
a soldier in his father's organization or not.

Heaven help her, she didn't care. All that mattered was that she loved him. And she was going to lose him.

"Chiara? Can you do that? Can you put your trust in me for this?"

She wanted to weep. Or rise from her chair and fling herself into her Raffaele's arms.

"*Sì,*" she whispered.

He smiled and said they had to be driving their poor waiter crazy, and would she like him to order for her? Chiara nodded because she didn't trust herself to speak.

If she did, she would say words he didn't want to hear, that she loved him...

That she would always love him, and treasure these days that she had been his wife.

Halfway through the meal, Rafe realized he'd never phoned his PA to tell her he'd be coming in today.

He'd ignored his schedule all week, but at least he'd phoned her each morning to say he wouldn't be in.

He hadn't even thought of phoning her today.

He'd had other things on his mind this morning, and just remembering those other things made him want to sweep Chiara into his arms, carry her off and make love to her. Make love with her. Make her come, and this time, when she cried out his name, he'd tell her—he'd tell her—

The floor seemed to tilt.

Tell her what?

All at once it seemed hard to breathe.

What had happened to all last night's resolutions? He was too old to let sex, even great sex, muddle his head. As for what he'd planned, taking Chiara to the Orsini offices... He had to be out of his mind!

What would he have said to his brothers? How would he have introduced her? Good morning, how are you guys today and, by the way, this is my wife?

Aside from anything else, what was the point? Why would it matter if she saw him as a respectable banker or went on believing he was a thug with a good wardrobe? Yes, he was...he was fond of her. He enjoyed being with her. But the whole arrangement, this supposed marriage, had the staying power of a dandelion in a windstorm.

Rafe blew out a long, hard breath.

Wow.

All that stuff about not digging yourself further

into a hole? He'd come within inches of burying himself so deep that getting out would have required a bulldozer.

Thank God he'd come to his senses.

He'd hail a cab, have it drive by the office, point the place out to Chiara. She could reach whatever conclusion she liked about him and his choice of occupations. Then he'd kiss her because, yeah, the sex was great. But that didn't mean he had to explain himself to her. So he'd kiss her, step out of the cab, go to work, let the cabbie take her back uptown. Once he was in his office, he'd phone Sayers's office. If she was back, fine. If not, who gave a damn if her partner creaked when he walked? Hell, a divorce was just a divorce. Any attorney could handle it.

What a relief, that he could suddenly see things with such clarity. He'd been in a fog the past few days, but the fog had lifted, the sun was out—

"More coffee?" the waiter said.

"No," Rafe replied. Chiara looked at him in surprise. Had he sounded a little brusque? Maybe, but suddenly he was a man in a hurry. How could he have let things get so far out of hand? "I just realized," he told her, "that I have a couple of appointments later this morning."

She nodded. Her face lost a little of its animation but she put her napkin beside her plate and rose to her feet before he could even get to his.

"Or course," she said politely. "You must work today."

"Yes, that's right. So, we'll just drive by my place—"

"It is not necessary, Raffaele."

"No. We'll drive by. Then, uh, then you can go back to the apartment while I—"

His voice trailed away as he peeled off a bunch of bills and dropped them on the table, too much in a rush, now that he'd come to his senses, to waste time waiting for the check.

A taxi pulled to the curb as they stepped into the street. As soon as its passengers got out, Rafe reached for the door and motioned Chiara in. He got in after her, gave the driver the address and sat back. He'd held her hand all the way downtown. Now he sat with his arms folded, saying nothing.

Chiara was silent, too. He glanced at her once. She was pale. It made him feel lousy. The cab pulled to the curb. Rafe looked out the window at the familiar building. It had a cast-iron facade, typical of many of the old buildings in the area, adorned with graceful arches and friezes. He and his brothers had put hundreds of thousands of dollars into restoring it; it had been named a New York City landmark and featured in half a dozen architectural magazines after the work was completed. He was proud of it—they all were—and he realized now he'd been hoping Chiara would like it, hell, that she'd find it charming, but what did that matter? What did her likes, her dislikes, her thoughts about him have to do with anything?

She was not part of his life.

He didn't want her as part of his life.

He wanted out of this mess. This marriage. This ridiculous situation...

"Damn it all," he growled, and when Chiara looked at him, her eyes blurry with tears, Rafe pulled her into his arms.

He kissed her hard. Kissed her deep. She kissed him back the same way, her hands clutching at his shoulders, her tears salty on his lips.

The cabby cleared his throat. "Uh, you want to get out, mister? Or you want to keep going?"

Laughter bubbled from Chiara's lips. Rafe grinned and leaned his forehead against hers.

"See this building?" he said softly.

She looked out and nodded. "It is a beautiful building, Raffaele."

"Yeah, well, it's mine." His voice was gruff with the pride that comes of knowing you've forged a place in the world and that you did it on your own. "Ours. My brothers and me. Dante, Falco and Nicolo. We're in business together. See that brass plaque above the door? Orsini Brothers. We're private bankers. Financial advisors. Brokers. Not one of us followed in our father's footsteps. You understand?" He cupped her face in his hands. "You didn't marry a saint, Chiara, but you didn't marry a crook, either. You married—you married me."

Her smile lit her entire face.

"I am glad," she said softly.

"Yeah," he said gruffly. "Me, too."

Rafe drew her close in his arms, gave the driver his Fifth Avenue address, and took his wife home.

A private elevator was a fine thing.

It meant a man could kiss his wife as soon as the door shut, and by the time the door opened again, he could have her half-undressed. It meant he could lift her in his arms, carry her into his living room, tear off his own clothes and the rest of hers and then make love to her on a white silk sofa with the warmth of the midday sun on them both.

Rafe lingered over Chiara's every curve. No inch of skin went unkissed. He lavished attention on her breasts, sucking the nipples deep into his mouth, then gently spread her thighs and gave her clitoris that same intense care. And while she was sobbing from her first orgasm, he turned her on her belly, kissed the nape of her neck, the sensitive places behind her ears, stroked his hand down her spine, followed that same path with his lips, then cupped his hand between her legs, groaning with pleasure at how her body wept with desire for him, for his penetration.

"Please," his wife whispered, "Raffaele, please…"

He eased her onto her knees. Slid slowly, slowly inside her, his hands cupping her breasts, his breathing harsh as he fought for control. She cried out as her second orgasm took her. Then, only then, Rafe let go, let his control shatter, his emotions soar as the truth filled him with almost unbearable joy.

He was in love with his wife.

* * *

After, he opened a bottle of Châteauneuf du Pape and poured glasses of the rich, red wine for them both.

Though it was fall, it was not really cool enough for a fire. Still, he built one in the massive stone fireplace, dumped a couple of fat couch pillows in front of it, wrapped his wife and himself in a black cashmere afghan and sat holding her in his arms as they watched the flames and drank the wine.

The knowledge that he loved her weighed inside him.

He had not wanted Chiara, because his father had ordered him to want her. Now he wanted her with all his heart—but what if she didn't want him?

What if she wanted the quick divorce he'd promised her? Yes, that was before all the rest, the hours in each other's arms, but he wasn't a boy, he was a man. He knew damned well making love wasn't the same as being in love.

She'd lived the life of a fairy-tale Rapunzel, locked away in a castle. She'd been lonely. Innocent. Afraid of being given to a man who was an ogre. He'd come along and changed all that. If he told her he loved her, she might feel grateful enough to say she loved him, too, and gratitude was the last thing he wanted.

What if he wanted her…and she wanted her freedom?

When had things become so complicated?

He looked down at his wife, lying peacefully in his embrace, her head against his naked chest, her eyes half-closed, the dark lashes curved against her cheeks. His heart swelled with love.

Why was he trying to work this like an equation? He had to tell her what he felt, just say, "Chiara, sweetheart, I don't want a divorce. I want you. I need you. I love—"

The intercom buzzed.

Rafe frowned. Who could it be? He certainly wasn't expecting anyone.

Chiara looked at him. "Raffaele? What is that?"

"It's nothing, sweetheart. Just the intercom. It'll stop after a—"

Bzzzz.

Ah-ha. The Saks delivery. Rafe bit back a smile, kissed the top of her head and eased her off his lap. "It's the doorman. Must be a delivery. He's authorized to sign for me but…" He smiled. "I'll be right back."

But it wasn't a delivery. It was, the doorman

said, his brothers. Two of them, anyway. They had their own elevator keys and they'd gone straight by him. In fact, they were pressing the call bell right now and considering that Mr. Orsini and his lady guest had, um, had gone upstairs rather hastily.

Rafe slammed down the phone. He could hear the gentle hum of the car starting its descent. Bewildered, he ran his hand through his hair. Two of his brothers. Nicolo and Falco, probably, unless Dante was back in town and—and what in hell did that matter? His brothers were on their way.

And Chiara was naked in his living room.

He ran to her. Took her hand and pulled her to her feet.

"Raffaele?"

"It's okay," he said as they raced up the stairs. "It's just that my brothers are here."

Her gasp almost suctioned all the air out of the stairwell. *"Dio mio!* Your brothers? But we are—"

"Right." He shouldered open the door to his room, almost broke his neck tripping over the dozens of boxes and shopping bags piled on the floor. "I haven't told them anything about— I haven't said a word to anyone about—" He took a breath. "Just get dressed, baby, okay? I'll handle the rest."

"Get dressed in what? This is not my room, it is yours."

"Yeah. Okay, but there's stuff here." He gestured at the packages. "The things you tried on this morning."

"You bought it all?"

"Yes. So just grab something and—"

"But I told you—"

"This is no time to argue!" Rafe hurried into his dressing room, yanked on a pair of jeans, tugged a T-shirt over his head and heard Nick's voice drifting up the stairs.

"Rafe? Are you up there, man?"

Chiara froze. So did he. "Raffaele?" she whispered.

Rafe shook his head, held up his hand. "I'll be right down."

"We'll come up if—"

"No! No, that's okay. I'm on my way."

"Raffaele." His wife was the color of cream. "My clothes…they are all over the living room!"

So were his. Damn. It was face-the-music time. A couple of minutes from now his brothers would know all about Chiara. That he had gone to Italy, that he had married her against his better judgment…

That he loved her.

The timing sucked. They'd know that last part before she did but what the hell, if there was one thing life had taught him, it was that you played the cards you were dealt even if they weren't the ones you'd have preferred.

He took a couple of breaths, then went to the door.

"Raffaele, wait!"

Chiara flew to him, wrapped her arms around his neck, rose on her toes and kissed him. He took her by the wrists and drew her hands to her sides.

"We have to talk."

He sounded more serious than she had ever heard him sound. The look in his eyes was serious, too. A chill swept through her.

"Talk about what, Raffaele?"

She saw his Adam's apple move as he swallowed.

"About us." He lifted his hand as if he might cup her cheek but he didn't. Instead he headed for the stairs.

CHAPTER FOURTEEN

FALCO and Nick were on the terrace, deep in conversation.

Rafe knew they were talking about him. He hadn't gone to the office in over a week. He'd shown up at The Bar and behaved like a crazy man, and today, again, he hadn't shown up at work.

Yeah. Well, okay. The sooner he told them what was going on, the better.

First he'd get rid of that telltale pile of clothes by the sofa. Maybe they hadn't noticed it. He could just grab the stuff, like this, open a door of the built-in sound system and jam it all inside.

Good. Excellent. Now take another deep breath—he was becoming an expert at those—and join them on the terrace.

"Hi," he said brightly.

His brothers turned toward him. They looked grim.

"Great idea, coming out here," he said so

cheerfully that he felt like a TV commercial. "The sun, the blue sky—"

"What's going on?" Falco said.

"Going on?"

"You heard him," Nick said. "What's the deal with you?"

"No deal." This was going to be harder than he'd thought. "I just...I just—"

"You haven't come to the office in days."

Falco's tone annoyed him. "What, I need a note from Mama saying why I'm absent?"

"Are you sick?"

"Am I—?" Rafe shook his head. They were worried about him, was all. His expression softened. "No, Nicolo. I'm not."

Nick and Falco exchanged looks. Then Nick reached into the pocket of his suit jacket.

"You left this in the elevator."

He looked at what was in Nick's hand. Hell. Chiara's white cotton panties. He'd forgotten to tell the clerk at Saks to provide his wife with lingerie, but it didn't matter; there was something about all that innocent white cotton that—

"Rafe?"

His head came up. Nick's eyebrows were raised. So were Falco's.

"Yeah," he mumbled, and grabbed the panties from his brother.

"Either you've taken to cross-dressing," Falco said calmly, "or more than the elevator was going down."

Another time Rafe would have laughed. Now he was too busy trying to stuff the panties into his pocket.

"Very amusing."

"Does this have to do with that woman you said was staying here?"

"No. Yes." Rafe glared at Nick. "Hey, man, what is this? An interrogation?"

His brothers looked at each other again.

"It's called brotherly concern," Falco said wryly. "It's what happens when you have a brother who's always behaved a certain way and all of a sudden he begins doing stuff that doesn't make sense."

"Look, I'm fine. Okay? I'm not a kid. And—"

"We're worried about you, man."

Rafe's righteous indignation vanished. They *were* worried. He could see it. Besides, putting this off wouldn't make the telling any easier.

"Yeah." He cleared his throat. "Uh, anybody for a beer?"

"No," Falco growled.

Nick gave him a sharp elbow in the ribs. "Beer sounds good."

Falco glared at him. Nick shrugged his shoulders, raised his eyebrows, did everything he could to transmit the message. Back off. Give him time. Don't crowd him. Okay?

A muscle ticked in Falco's jaw. He was not good at backing off, but after a couple of seconds he nodded.

"Beer's fine."

The brothers marched into the kitchen. Nick almost tripped over a woman's high-heeled boot. He grinned, gave Falco another elbow. Falco looked, grinned, but then the two of them frowned.

The situation might have been funny, but it wasn't. They had come here worried that Rafe was sick. Now they knew whatever was wrong with him had something to do with a woman. A woman for whom he'd lost a week's worth of appointments. A woman he was so hot for he'd undressed her in his elevator. Okay, sure, each of them had done the elevator bit or something close to it, but for one of them to change the very pattern of his life…

Not good. Not good at all.

They took the cold, sweating bottles of beer Rafe took from the Sub-Zero fridge. Opened the bottles, drank, wiped the backs of their hands across their mouths, gave him time, gave him time, gave him—

"I got married."

Nick's beer bottle slipped through his hand. He made a last-minute grab and caught it, but not before half its contents spilled on his shoes. The bottle in Falco's hand tilted, sending a waterfall of beer down the front of his suit.

"You what?"

Rafe raised his shoulders, let them drop.

"I got married. A week ago."

Nick looked at Falco. "He got married."

Falco nodded. "The white underpants."

"He married a woman who wears white—"

"Okay," Rafe said coldly, "that's enough. We're not going to do a comedy riff on my wife's underwear."

Silence. Then Nick cleared his throat. "Fine. What we'd really like to discuss is your wife."

Rafe hesitated. Then he gave another of those shrugs. "Yeah. I just— The thing is, I don't know where to start."

"The beginning almost always works," Falco said quietly.

Rafe nodded. He put his bottle of beer on the counter. His brothers did the same. Then they wandered into the living room, sat down, and Rafe began to talk.

He did as Falco had suggested. Began at the beginning, at the meeting called by their father.

"The old man was at his best," he said grimly. "He didn't just talk about dying, he talked about his soul."

His brothers snorted. "What soul?" Nick said.

"I told him that, but he insisted he'd done something years ago, in Sicily, and now he had to make up for it."

"And what did that have to do with you? For that matter, what does it have to do with your getting married?"

"He said the only way to make up for what he'd done was for me to go to San Giuseppe—"

"Where he was born?"

"Right. He wanted me to go there and marry the daughter of a Sicilian *don*."

"And you told him what he could do with that request," Falco said.

"I did. I told him there was no way in the world I'd do it. Trouble was, I'd already given my word that I'd help him with the immortal soul nonsense." Rafe paused, tried to pretend his brothers weren't looking at him as if he'd lost his mind. "So I said, okay, I'd fly to Sicily but I sure as hell wasn't marrying anybody."

"Then, how'd you end up marrying this—this hoodlum princess?"

"She's not," Rafe said sharply. "She'd not anything like that."

"Sorry," Falco said coolly. "How'd you end up putting a ring on a stranger's finger?"

Rafe laughed. "Actually, I haven't. Not yet. It was—it was a kind of quick thing, you know? See, what happened was…"

Was what?

He thought about how Chiara had waylaid him on the road from Palermo. He thought of the first time he'd kissed her. They didn't need to hear all that. It was too personal, too much a part of what he and his wife had immediately felt for each other and tried to deny. Instead, he told them the only part that counted. The ultimatum handed down by her father, that if Rafe didn't marry her, he would give her to his brute of a *capo*.

Nick swore softly.

Rafe nodded. "I didn't have any choice. I said I'd marry her. And I did."

"You had a choice," Falco said. "You could have walked away."

"Would you?"

Falco gave him a long, assessing look. Then he shrugged. "Okay. You married her. Brought her to the States. And then what? Surely you told her you weren't doing this for real."

"Of course!" Rafe dug his hands into the back pockets of his jeans and began to pace. "Would I marry a woman I didn't choose for myself? Would I marry a woman because Cesare demanded it?"

"Hell, no."

"I made it clear this whole thing was temporary."

"You called your lawyer?"

"Sayers. Sure. I called her right away." Rafe shook his head. "She's been out of the country. She told me to call the guy covering for her."

"And you did."

"No. I didn't." Telling the story was almost as complicated as living it. "I thought I'd wait for Sayers to come home…but things began to change."

"The white-panties-in-the-elevator kind of change," Nick said mildly.

Rafe swung toward him, glaring. "I told you that wasn't up for discussion."

"Maybe it should be. You took the lady to bed. You turned a logistical problem into an emotional one," Falco said coldly.

"No. Yes. Damn it, it's not that simple!"

"Isn't it?"

"I knew what I had to do. Be supportive. Help her get started. Find her a place to live, that kind of thing."

"But?"

"But it was all easier said than done. I felt responsible for her." He paused. "And then, just a little while ago, I got it all sorted out."

"Thank God for small favors," Falco muttered.

"I realized I'd been dancing around, refusing to deal with reality."

Nick rolled his eyes. "Hallelujah."

"And now, I know exactly what I have to do."

"Then do it."

"I was going to. I was going to talk to Chiara, tell her the truth—but you two bozos showed up."

"So, you'll tell her after we leave."

"Of course I will. But, see, it isn't that easy." Rafe turned and paced the room again, then swung toward his brothers. "She knows I wanted out. I was up-front about it right from the start. Hell, I said it every chance I could. I didn't want her misunderstanding our deal. But—"

"But you've slept with her," Falco said bluntly. "And that complicated things."

"Did you hear what I said? It isn't that simple."

"Sure it is. You're worried about how she'll react when you tell her the truth."

"Damn it, of course I'm worried! What if she doesn't react the way I want her to react? What if she says no? What if she says, 'Raffaele, I married you. And now—'"

"And now," a female voice said, "and now, it is over."

The three men swung around. Nick and Falco blinked. The woman who stood halfway down the steps was dressed all in black. Her hair was pulled back in a bun and she was carrying a black overnight bag.

"Chiara." Rafe smiled and started toward her. "Baby. I'm glad you're here. I want you to meet my—"

"I have no interest in meeting these men."

Chiara's tone was frigid. A good thing, because her pulse was racing so fast that the room was spinning. If she sounded cold, sounded controlled, perhaps she would not weep. Perhaps her Raffaele would never know that he had broken her heart.

"Sweetheart. These are my broth—"

"I left the things I wore on the bed, Raffaele. I am sure you can give them to charity."

Rafe blinked. What in hell was happening? Why was his Chiara dressed like this? Why was she looking at him through such cold eyes? He'd just been about to tell his brothers that he was in love with his wife, that he was terrified of telling her he loved her because she might say that was all very nice but she wanted her freedom, just as he'd promised.

"Baby. What's this all about?"

"Do not call me that. And do not treat me as if I were stupid. I assure you, I am not."

Rafe stepped in front of her as she came down the rest of the steps. "Chiara…"

"Please get out of my way."

Her chin rose. Her eyes glittered with unshed tears. She was, once again, his tough yet vulnerable Chiara. And though he didn't understand the reason, she was making it clear she didn't want him.

His eyes narrowed. "What's going on here?"

"The truth. That is what is going on here. You and your brothers have no need to worry. I do not want this marriage. I never did. I want a divorce, as we agreed, and I want it as fast as possible."

"Chiara—"

"I heard everything," she said, and felt her composure slipping. "I heard every word, Raffaele!'

"You heard…? No. Wait a minute. See, you misunderstood. What I was telling my brothers was that… Chiara!" Rafe's voice rose as she swept past him and ran not to the elevator but to the kitchen.

Okay. At least she hadn't left. All he had to do was get rid of Nick and Falco and talk to her, get her to listen…

The kitchen?

"Damn it," Rafe said, "the service entrance!"

Falco grabbed his arm. "Raffaele. Let her go."

"Damn you, let go of me!"

"Rafe," Nick said. "Okay, she got the last laugh. So what? Who cares who made the first move? You wanted her gone. Well, she's gone. Give it a couple of days, a week, you'll forget this little scene ever—"

Rafe wrenched free of Falco's hand.

"You idiots," he roared. "I didn't want her gone! I love her. I'll always love her. She's my *wife*!"

Nicolo and Falco looked at each other as Rafe raced into the kitchen. The service door stood open. Beyond it the lights above the service elevator showed that it had already reached the basement.

"*Cazzo!*" Falco said.

"You got that right," Nick said.

Then they took off after Rafe, who was already pounding down the fire stairs.

Chiara burst into the street and stopped in confusion.

She was on an unfamiliar side street. Then she heard the blare of a horn, looked toward the corner and saw that she was a few hundred feet from Fifth Avenue and its taxis and buses. She had no money for either but that was a problem she'd handle when she had to.

She began to run.

What a fool she'd been! This afternoon, lying in Raffaele's arms, her heart filled with love, she'd indulged in a little fantasy, let herself think that what she saw in his eyes was more than desire, that it was love.

"*Idiota,*" she said, and she ran faster.

He didn't love her. Why would he? She'd been

an encumbrance that had changed into a sex toy. Very nice for him, but then, sex was what men were all about. She knew that, she had *always* known that. How could she have forgotten?

"Chiara!"

It was his voice. Her Raffaele was running after her, but he wasn't "her" Raffaele anymore, he wasn't "her" anything.

"Chiara! Wait!"

She had the advantage of a head start but his legs were longer. He would catch her; it was just a matter of time. She was on Fifth Avenue now. There were taxis whizzing by and she ran into the street, waving her hand wildly, but she might as well have been invisible. The cabs kept going.

"Chiara!"

She looked back. *Dio!* His brothers were just behind him. She had to do something!

Chiara dove into the snarl of traffic, ignoring the blasting horns, the squeal of brakes. She heard Raffaele shout after her again, and then, mercifully, she was in the park.

Running was easier here.

No cars. No buses. Pedestrians, but she raced past them. She was a good runner. She had strong legs from years of tromping the hills outside San Giuseppe. If she could just put some real distance between her and—

Raffaele grabbed her from behind.

She yelped, his legs tangled with hers and they went down in a heap. She tried to roll away but he had her on her back, his hips straddling hers, his hands clasping her fists. Now his brothers were there, too, disheveled and panting and looking down at her with anger in their eyes.

"Let me go!" she demanded.

Raffaele stood up and dragged her to her feet.

"I said, let—me—go!"

"Never," he growled, and the hard look in his face made her shudder.

"I will scream—"

"No. You won't," he said, and covered her mouth with his.

Chiara beat her fists against her husband's powerful shoulders. She nipped at his lip. And then, even though it was disgraceful to do it, she gave herself up to this one last kiss.

And then another. And another...

"Uh, Rafe? You need us, buddy?"

Rafe didn't answer. Instead he framed his

Chiara's face with his hands, changed the angle of the kiss and felt his heart take a tentative leap when she gave one of those little moans.

"He doesn't need us," Falco said.

"No," Nick said, laughing, "he doesn't."

They wished him luck, said they'd really like to meet the little woman if the two of them ever came up for air—

And then they were gone.

"I love you," Rafe whispered against his wife's lips.

"No," she said brokenly, "you do not. I heard every word you said."

"You couldn't have, because I never had the chance to say the only words that mattered." Rafe held her away from him, just far enough so he could see her beloved face. "I love you, Chiara."

"But you said you didn't know how to tell me you wanted to end our marriage. You said—"

"I said I didn't know how to tell you I loved you. At least, that was what I was going to say." Rafe smiled. "You just didn't give me the chance."

"Oh, Raffaele. Be sure. Please, be sure… because I love you. I adore you. I—"

Rafe kissed her again. This was New York, and

people were detouring around them, but even some of those hardened New Yorkers smiled.

"I love you," Rafe said. "I don't ever want to lose you. I want you to be my wife, forever." He swallowed hard. "That is, if you'll have me."

Chiara laughed, even though tears still shone in her eyes.

"I will have you for all the rest of our lives, my Raffaele," she said, and her husband swept her into his arms. Those hardened New Yorkers whistled and cheered, and Raffaele Orsini carried home his beautiful, tempestuous bride.

Not every man got to marry the same woman twice.

Rafe did.

When he broke the news of his marriage to his family, everyone went a little crazy.

His mother wept. His sisters, too. Falco and Nicolo, who, of course, already knew all about it, rolled their eyes at the unseemly commotion. Dante, who'd been clued in on his return from only he knew where, shrugged and flashed a cryptic smile.

Cesare just looked smug and said he had known it would happen. Rafe decided to leave it at that. His father had meddled in his life, not to benefit his son but to salve his own conscience. That things had worked out changed nothing.

"A wedding," his mother said, drying her eyes on her apron. "We must have a *real* wedding."

Rafe said they'd already had one, but his sisters took up the chant, and when he looked at his wife, he saw that her eyes were shining at the very idea. So he did what men always do in such situations.

He gave in.

The ceremony took place in the little neighborhood church Sofia Orsini had always loved. Either the Feds and the cops were kind that day or they simply kept a low profile, but there wasn't an agent or a police officer in sight.

Chiara wore a gown of antique French lace over silk. Tiny pink silk rosebuds adorned the train, and Sofia's wedding veil fell gracefully from a tiara of pink roses in her dark hair.

"Cesare and I eloped," Sofia said shyly, "but my mama knew our plan and gave me her veil. I would be honored if you wore it."

Chiara wept a little, kissed her mother-in-law and said it was she who would be honored.

Anna and Isabella were her maids of honor.

Nick, Falco and Dante were Rafe's best men. It made for a crowd at the altar. The men grinned, the women giggled, but everyone grew solemn once the simple ceremony began.

"My Chiara," Rafe whispered when it was time to lift his bride's veil and kiss her.

She smiled into his eyes. "My Raffaele," she said softly, and kissed him with all the love in her heart.

Afterward, at the reception, Isabella and Anna happily agreed it had all been like a fairy tale.

There were no fairy tales, Dante thought grimly, not for him, anyway…. But he wisely decided to keep that bit of information to himself.

MILLS & BOON PUBLISH EIGHT LARGE PRINT TITLES A MONTH. THESE ARE THE EIGHT TITLES FOR FEBRUARY 2010.

DESERT PRINCE, BRIDE OF INNOCENCE
Lynne Graham

RAFFAELE: TAMING HIS TEMPESTUOUS VIRGIN
Sandra Marton

THE ITALIAN BILLIONAIRE'S SECRETARY MISTRESS
Sharon Kendrick

BRIDE, BOUGHT AND PAID FOR
Helen Bianchin

BETROTHED: TO THE PEOPLE'S PRINCE
Marion Lennox

THE BRIDESMAID'S BABY
Barbara Hannay

THE GREEK'S LONG-LOST SON
Rebecca Winters

HIS HOUSEKEEPER BRIDE
Melissa James

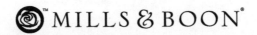

MILLS & BOON PUBLISH EIGHT LARGE PRINT TITLES A MONTH. THESE ARE THE EIGHT TITLES FOR MARCH 2010.

—————————— ⚮ ——————————

A BRIDE FOR HIS MAJESTY'S PLEASURE
Penny Jordan

THE MASTER PLAYER
Emma Darcy

THE INFAMOUS ITALIAN'S SECRET BABY
Carole Mortimer

THE MILLIONAIRE'S CHRISTMAS WIFE
Helen Brooks

CROWNED: THE PALACE NANNY
Marion Lennox

CHRISTMAS ANGEL FOR THE BILLIONAIRE
Liz Fielding

UNDER THE BOSS'S MISTLETOE
Jessica Hart

JINGLE-BELL BABY
Linda Goodnight

millsandboon.co.uk Community

Join Us!

The Community is the perfect place to meet and chat to kindred spirits who love books and reading as much as you do, but it's also the place to:

- **Get the inside scoop from authors about their latest books**
- **Learn how to write a romance book with advice from our editors**
- **Help us to continue publishing the best in women's fiction**
- **Share your thoughts on the books we publish**
- **Befriend other users**

Forums: Interact with each other as well as authors, editors and a whole host of other users worldwide.

Blogs: Every registered community member has their own blog to tell the world what they're up to and what's on their mind.

Book Challenge: We're aiming to read 5,000 books and have joined forces with The Reading Agency in our inaugural Book Challenge.

Profile Page: Showcase yourself and keep a record of your recent community activity.

Social Networking: We've added buttons at the end of every post to share via digg, Facebook, Google, Yahoo, technorati and de.licio.us.

www.millsandboon.co.uk